FILTH 末族

Failed in London, Try Hong Kong

Jingan MacPherson Young

香港藝術節委約及製作
Commissioned & produced by the Hong Kong Arts Festival

Foreword

The 42nd HKAF is filled with heroes: patriotic outlaws and a tiger-quelling young warrior, lovers fighting societal norms, a mysterious knight in shining armour, and a doubtful death-defying magician. There are also heroes of dance and heroic journeys in music. In this company of heroes, we must count two young playwrights whose work you can enjoy both on stage and in the pages that follow.

Since embarking on production and publication of local theatre, we have worked exclusively in Chinese thus far. This year, we mark another milestone in doing the first English language production, addressing a sector that is somewhat underserved in a bilingual city. I hope that other works will follow in the years to come.

I salute both playwrights: Wang Haoran and Young Jingan, and the many artists whose talent and artistry lend lustre to the 42nd HKAF. I also salute our audiences and the many partners and supporters whose contributions make the Festival possible. Above all, I salute my HKAF colleagues. Their energy and dedication inform my understanding of what it means to be a hero on a daily basis, and it is a privilege to be in their company.

Tisa Ho
Executive Director, Hong Kong Arts Festival

Playwright's Notes

The instinctual "thrill of the hunt", one may argue, can be likened to that of the dramatist in search of a good story. Amid the hyperreality of skyscrapers and sampans, my upbringing became synonymous with the phrase "in pursuit of" and so, to theatricalize the everyday (asides from the vain attempt to make sense of the madness) inevitably became the recurrent theme to which my play's heroes convey their dissatisfaction with the world around them. Perhaps the greatest, if not exhaustive subject explored within modern theatre (and life too).

But this is drama (my favourite kind). It is "a living art". It has a heartbeat, a soul, no one performance like the next. Theatre can inspire, teach, entertain and like most things, has a tendency to break your heart.

"Language is a skin," Roland Barthes said. One may apply this sentiment to the little-known acronym *FILTH* – "Failed in London, Try Hong Kong" – a term the privileged few who emigrated from Britain to our ex-colony in the South China Sea were either christened with, or affixed to themselves as a badge of honour. The etymology of the word is vague. The story is not.

This city has undergone monumental changes since the Handover of 1997. The politics of which I have woven into these characters' lives, albeit a decade later. The play's backcloth, that is, Hong Kong's ambivalent future is symbolic.

Love, sex and power are all "beaten out on a native drum". The question is how and when do these two paths converge? Are they mutually exclusive? We cannot foresee the future, only glimpses. We cannot proclaim, only prophesize.

I am indebted to the Hong Kong Arts Festival who without none of this would be possible. I am honoured this play was chosen as the Festival's first English language commission and my greatest hope is this trilingual play will open the door for new playwrights in Hong Kong.

Dedicated to my parents

 Young was born in Hong Kong on the 18th October 1990. She holds a Bachelor of Arts (Honours) in English with Film Studies from Kings College London (2012) and a Master of Studies in Creative Writing at Oxford University (2014). She is the first playwright commissioned in English by the Hong Kong Arts Festival for *FILTH* (Failed in London, Try Hong Kong) in the 42nd HKAF. She is a graduate of The Royal Court Theatre's Young Writers Programme (2011) and of the Hampstead Theatre's youth company Heat & Light (2011). She has won bursaries from BAFTA, BBC and ScriptFactory UK (2009- 2011) for screenwriting. Her plays have been performed in The Hampstead Theatre Downstairs (*Moira* 2011), Jacksons Lane (*The Eyes Have It*' 2009), Anatomy Theatre & Museum (*The T-group* 2013) and The Keble O'Reilly Theatre (*Antigone* 2013). She is also a regular contributor to the *South China Morning Post*.

FILTH premiered at the 42nd Hong Kong Arts Festival,
Theatre, Hong Kong City Hall,
14 March, 2014.

Characters and Premiere Cast

Joe Losey	Charlie Schroeder
Rebecca Losey / Angelique	Nina Kwok
Ricky Forrester	David Peatfield
Elaine	Nicole Russo
Fanny	Wong Ching-yan Birdy
Ah Fung	Yuen Fu Wah
Hitler	Ryan Lam-decker / Matthew Wong
Playwright	Jingan MacPherson Young
Director	Peter Jordan
Set Designer	Yoki Lai
Lighting Designer	Billy Chan
Costume Designer	Cheng Man-wing
Music and Sound Designer	Sham Chung-tat
Production Manager	Gloria Ngai
Producer	Hong Kong Arts Festival

Cover photographs © Calvin Sit: (from left to right)
Nicole Russo, Charlie Schroeder, Nina Kwok, David Peatfield

Setting

Hong Kong. 1st July 2007.

Characters

Joe Losey, English, thirties
Rebecca Losey, Eurasian, thirties
Angelique, played by the same actress as Rebecca, thirties
Ricky Forrestor, Australian, thirties
Elaine, English, thirties
Fanny, Hong Kong Chinese, twenty
Ah Fung, Hong Kong Chinese, forties
Hitler, ten

Scenes

Act One Renovations

Act Two Revolutions

Act Three Revelations

Generally dialogue is spoken very quickly but concisely. Characters hide behind words - their preferred weapon of choice.

(/) indicates the next speech begins from that point.
(-) indicates the next line interrupts.
(...) means the speech trails off signaling the character is in hesitation or expectation.
[ ] means the voice over speaking by the character
A line with no full stop indicates the next speech begins immediately.

Note on translations

Whether Fanny and Ah Fung's exchanges are in Cantonese or English is purely down to preference of production. Their commentary, which cannot be understood by English characters, is marked "(in Cantonese.)" One method of translation could be to have a scrolling bar affixed somewhere on stage. Where there is "Hong Kong Chinese English" (Chinglish), words should be sounded out the way they appear.

FILTH

"Failed in London, Try Hong Kong."

Act **1**

Renovations

ACT ONE

Prologue

Joe and Rebecca Losey's flat currently under renovation.

Everything is covered. There are paint buckets and small cement mixers on the carpet. Modern, expensively furnished, impersonal and sterile. To the right - unfinished open plan kitchen.

Large balcony upstage provides a panoramic view of Victoria Harbour. Doors leading to the bedrooms should also be visible.

Spotlight on Joe (suited) who stumbles in from the bedroom carrying a bottle of Champagne. He takes a swig, collapses onto the sofa.

Angelique (played by the same actress as Rebecca) enters from the bedroom wearing only Joe's jacket. Joe stands, walks towards her, trips, falls. She switches on a nearby lamp. She grabs the bottle, pours it onto his face. He wakes, splutters...

Joe: Rebecca?

She helps him back onto the sofa, extracts a packet of Cocaine. She cuts a line. She stands, moves her hips to the beat - Joe remains expressionless.

Strobe lights glitter. We hear the heavy bass of a club remix. We hear the sounds, news feeds & interviews from the Handover of 1997 along with Ricky Forrester's radio programme. The sounds slowly build to a deafening crescendo whilst Angelique continues to gyrate.

[Tony Blair] "A new dawn has broken, has it not?"

Joe does a line - lies back.

[Ricky] "You're listening to the *Enquirer* news radio service with me Ricky Forrester."

Trading bell goes off in the distance. Ding Ding Ding.

[Ricky] "Ex-governor Chris 'Fatty Pang' Patten expressed his own concerns in yesterday's *Guardian*..."

Joe does another line.

[Chris Patten] "This is a cause for celebration, not sorrow."

Angelique removes Joe's shoes.

[Soldier] "Forward March!"

[Drum Roll]

[Ricky] "Ten years on. Re-birth? What a load of shite."

[Margaret Thatcher] "It's almost a miracle."

[Applause]

Angelique climbs into his lap.

[Prince Charles] "Her majesty the Queen...good wishes...staunch... special friends..."

[Princess Diana] "You always think you're the perfect everything."

Angelique removes Joe's tie.

[Static]

Lights begin to flicker violently...

[Thatcher] "We negotiated...we hope it will be upheld...again... again...again."

[Chris Patten] "Unshakeable destiny."

She grabs his face - roughly kisses him - nothing.

[Thatcher] "Again...again...again"

[Prince Charles] "We shall not forget you."

Stage is flooded with red light, the couple appear frozen in time...

[Prince Charles] "Forget you...forget you...forget you...forget you..."

[Ricky] "Fuck if I know whether it's better or worse since 1997."

Blackout

Quickly transition to...

Scene One

Months later. Late morning. Sunday 1 July 2007.

Losey's flat - still under renovation.

Sound of DRILLING and HAMMERING periodically.

The coffee table is now littered with equipment: a toolbox, a drill, a burning cigarette in a homemade tinfoil ashtray...

Hitler emerges (dressed in an English public school uniform and wearing an adult-sized chauffeur's cap). He skips around the flat treating it as his playground.

Hitler walks over to a tall cabinet on the other side of the room, on top there's a sealed cardboard box (marked "Rob Hunter: Editor" clearly visible to the audience). Hitler climbs onto a chair, reaches, the box topples over onto the ground. He rifles through it, pulls out a BB gun.

Fanny (clad in Hello Kitty T-shirt and sequined pink trainers) enters through the front door carrying a large carrier bag. Hitler quickly hides.

She dumps the keys and the bag on the coffee table, picks up the half-finished cigarette.

Fanny: Bunch of rich cunts!

Ah Fung stumbles in from the bedroom.

Ah Fung: Yo!

Fanny: Ah Fung, right?

Ah Fung: Nice shoes.

Fanny: Thanks. Look, I don't have a lot of time.

Ah Fung: Sure, sure.

Fanny: Where's your boss? Told me to pick this up. Bloody heavy whatever it is.

Hitler jumps on the sofa behind Fanny, waves the gun around, aims it behind her back...

Fanny: Where is she now?

Ah Fung stifles a laugh, shrugs -

Ah Fung: Around.

Fanny: Around? (beat.) What? What are you looking at?

Hitler pulls the trigger - click - no bullets fire - Fanny turns:

Fanny: Hey. Hey! What're you doing? Get down! Get down! I'm gonna be in so much shit! Please come down. Please! GET DOWN ALREADY! What are you...what *is* that? Give it to me! Give it to me!

Fanny attempts to grab the gun, Hitler resists and continues to click the trigger.

Ah Fung: Children, children! Cut it out will ya?

Fanny and Hitler struggle until...

The BB gun fires, a pellet hits Fanny's thigh.

Fanny: Aiyaaaaaaaaeeeeeeeyaaahhhhhhhhh!

She collapses onto the sofa. Ah Fung bursts into laughter. Hitler grabs the gun back.

Ah Fung: Hey, Hitler!

Hitler tosses the hat to Ah Fung, bows, exits.

Fanny: Ow ow ooh ow ow ow fuck ow ooh ow ow ow ow ow ooh ow fuck ow ow ow ow ow ooh.

Ah Fung: Could *really* use another fag.

Fanny: Little bastard!

Ah Fung: Getting too old for this shit.

Fanny: Ooh (beat.) Ooh (beat.) Ooh.

Ah Fung: You'll live

Fanny: Parents must be nuts, letting *that* off the leash!

Ah Fung: Some cultures consider shooting people with small copper balls character-building.

Fanny: What was he doing here anyway?

Ah Fung: You ask for too many questions.

Fanny lies down on the sofa.

Ah Fung: Didn't catch your name.

Fanny: Fanny.

Ah Fung: Why do you local girls always opt for variations on "cunt" as your Anglo name? If it ain't "Fanny", it'll be "Pussy", "Kitty", "Muffy". Remind me again "Fanny" what you are doing -

Fanny: I'm filling in for your regular. Uh, you know, the hobbling old dyke?

Ah Fung: Right right, yeah, "Amah". She's *"ill"*. Hee-hee-hee.

Fanny: What?

Ah Fung: Gonna have to find yourself a new job Fanny.

Drilling.

Fanny: WHAT?

Drilling stops.

Ah Fung: GONNA HAVE TO FIND A NEW JOB!

Fanny: No need to shout man! Unlike you, I hear *just* fine thanks very much. Why do I "need to find another job"?

Ah Fung: The Chinese, man! The Chinese! Beijing, Shanghai, Guangzhou. *They're* the ones with the big money now. Villagers giving one another high-fives off bruised backs, back-ended dealings between, what they "used" to proclaim "foreign scum", worn, weather-beaten shit-covered hands. Actually want us to *believe* this is the "New China"! I'd watch myself if I were you "Fanny". You're pretty, fertile, you might get lost in the shuffle.

Fanny: I'm taking a course at Vidal Sassoon.

Ah Fung: Last week for instance, she sacks practically all her employees, then goes and screws 'em all on TV...

Fanny: Who?

Ah Fung: Mrs. Losey.

Fanny: No way!

Ah Fung: *Way*

Fanny: She runs that newspaper, no?

Ah Fung: Inherited it from her father, probably turning in his grave. Her other half, Joe, crack-addict in a suit

Fanny: A what what?

Ah Fung: Banker.

Fanny: Oh, oh. Good One.

Ah Fung: He's been away for a while and by while I mean for like fucking forever.

Fanny: So?

Ah Fung: His best friend, Australian, works for Mrs. Losey. Real loser, "hippie" type, lives over on Lamma Island. He's been over here every night with her (beat.) alone.

Fanny: Really?

Ah Fung: They came here, think "I'll be a fucking billionaire in no time!" They're all the same. Same faces same voices same dreams same desires, never satisfied, "too hot, too humid." Ten years I've been driving this family. Ten years. Ten years. Ten bloody years! This family, you'd need a lifetime to...yeah I've got a bit of time, yeah, let me tell you a story Fanny.

Fanny: Okay...

Ah Fung: Rob Hunter, Mrs. Losey's father, he was close to the end, a whisper close to his last breath. Naturally I drove them to the hospital. They sat in the back of my car, well, their car, new beamer and I thought to myself, how clean they look, how white, how pristine. Nothing, not even death can touch them. Few minutes pass, sharp intake of breath and then Joe, Mr. Losey, told her, Mrs. Losey that he's got a last minute meeting (which I know for a fact is a big fat lie) standard, some ascension to bullshittery, can't stick around, flight to London's booked, "Ah Fung will take me to the airport directly".

Fanny: He just left?

Ah Fung: She doesn't say a word, just stares out. Joe continued to make his excuses, couldn't understand why she was being so unreasonable. We finally pulled into the car park. She opens the door herself, climbs out, walks in...

Fanny: And then?

Ah Fung: I drive him to the airport. Dad dies. Rebecca, she dies a little too. Every day.

Fanny: Wow. So, you think he's gone for good?

Ah Fung: Who knows? Losey's never had any kids. All this, this is all they have (beat.) ever had.

Fanny: Never been in a place like this before, except, you know, maybe the mall.

Ah Fung's mobile goes off.

Ah Fung: I'll be going now. Day off post-funeral thank fuck. You take care of yourself "Fanny". Oh and "Happy July 1st"!

Fanny: Whatever that means.

Fanny roots around the bag, it's a small basket, she opens it and peeks inside - an urn.

Fanny: Holy! Is that a, is this a...?

Ah Fung sees the urn - "bad luck" - immediately spits on the ground. He quickly closes the basket up.

Ah Fung: Great! Now I gotta change. *Again.*

Ah Fung puts on his hat, quickly makes his way to the door.

Ah Fung: Ten years! Place your bets now folks!

Ah Fung exists.

Fanny takes a tour of the room, picking up various objects and examining them. She then takes out her mobile and begins taking photos of herself.

After a few moments, Joe enters.

Joe: Hello?

Snap snap snap. Fanny continues to pose for the camera.

Joe: *Hello?*

Pause.

Fanny: Aiya...

Pause.

Fanny: Hallo.

Joe: Hello.

Fanny: Hallo hallo!

Joe moves to the kitchen. He takes out a pill bottle.

Joe: *Hello.* Look, who are you exactly?

He retrieves a beer from the fridge, washes the pills down.

Fanny: Who?

Joe: You.

Fanny: You?

Joe: You.

Fanny: You-ah?

Joe: *What* are you doing here?

Drilling.

Joe: (Loudly.) Why are you in my house?

Fanny: I (beat.) no (beat.) understand!

Joe: YOU.

Drilling stops.

Joe: WHO ARE YOU?

Fanny: (In Cantonese.) No need to shout. Flat-faced Gwei-Lo.

Joe: Ha-ha.

Fanny: Heh heh heh...?

Joe: I do know what a "Gwei-Lo" is. Straightforward, simple, derogatory, demeaning and very very funny way of referring to me, well "us". Am I the ghost man? Uncivilized bunch we are too what with our "foreign" ways, freedom of speech, binge drinking, self-deprecating humour...

Fanny: (In Cantonese.) Shit-faced foreigner. Look at your forehead. Size of a small planet.

Joe: Sorry?

Fanny: I dun understand!

Joe: Who *are* you?

Fanny: You?

Joe: You (slowly.) Who-are-you?

Fanny: Who are youuuuuuuuuu?

Joe: Good question. Who am I? Who the hell am I, really?

Fanny: Mista...Mista...

Joe: Yep. You got it. I'm "Mista Mista" of *all this*. Pretty neat huh? Tell me, as a member of the opposite sex, do you feel you hold this inescapable, innate need to renovate your place of residence every fortnight? Do you routinely, depending on the cycles of the moon, take a fancy to strip the sofas, rip up the walls, upholster the furniture? Be honest now.

Fanny: Mista Loo-zay!

Joe: Losey

Fanny: (Slowly.) Loo-zee

Joe: Call me Joe.

Fanny: Call-me-Joe?

Joe: Right. Joe. Call me Joe. What do I call you? What's, what's your name? (In Cantonese.) *Mat-yeah*...?

Fanny: Fanny-ah.

Joe: Where's Amah?

Fanny: Amah? What is Amah?

Joe: She's (beat.) never mind. How old are you anyway? No, *don't* tell me. Fuck, I'm old.

Fanny: Missus still out!

Joe: Thought as much.

Fanny: Dey tell me-ah, tonight is, how I say-ah, a, a partay? Big partay tonight. I pick dis all up for-ah partay but no tell me how many pe-poll go for partay so I get for "sap-go".

She holds up her palms, "number ten".

Joe: Missus doesn't have that many friends left, she must have meant four maybe, "sahm-wai?"

Joe mistakenly makes the "number four" gesture ["sahm" is Cantonese for number three].

Fanny: Ha. On-lyyy?

Joe: It'll be a great big fucking disaster.

Fanny: You want lunch? I make lunch?

Joe: I'm OK, thanks...

Fanny: You look so skinny la! I make chicken fried wice. You *love* chicken fried wice, hah?

23

Joe: (Laughs.) I *do* love but I already ate.

He gestures to his bags.

Fanny: Oh yes, you gone-ah so so long (beat.) Missus talk about you, uh, all time...

Joe: She did?

Fanny: Where you go? Norf Pole?

Joe: Not that far. Only London.

Fanny: I put away bag lata OK?

Joe: Thanks "Amah". Can I call you that? Amah? Can I call you Amah?

Fanny: OK OK. You go showa now? OK?

Joe: Good idea. I'm going to do just that. You carry on. Sorry...sorry if I disturbed you.

He exits to the bedroom. Fanny goes to the kitchen and gets out a vacuum cleaner. She looks around, coast is clear - she resumes taking photos of herself with her phone.

From the hallway:

Rebecca: (Offstage.) Bloody Sundays!

Elaine: (Offstage.) Keys?

Rebecca: (Offstage.) I bloody hate bloody

Fanny quickly turns on the vacuum cleaner.

Elaine: (Offstage.) *Keys.*

Elaine enters followed by Rebecca [both in black] laden with shopping bags full of food and wine.

Rebecca: Six months!

Elaine: Six months?

Rebecca: Finished, only so far as from here...to here.

Elaine: Potential though.

Rebecca: Potential "Potemkin Village" more like.

Elaine: What about tonight?

Rebecca: Who knows? Has someone been smoking in here?

Fanny turns off the vacuum cleaner.

Fanny: (In Cantonese.) *Jo-san!*

Rebecca: (Deadpan.) Yes. "Joe zaahhn".

Fanny beelines straight to Elaine.

Fanny: Hallo missus loo-zee. I finish cleaning here-ah but still bedwooms.

Rebecca: Over here.

Fanny: Hah?

Elaine: (In Mandarin.) This here, *he* is Mrs. Losey.

Fanny: Wah?

Rebecca: Yeah, what *she* said...

Elaine: Wang Feng

Rebecca: Wang Feng?

Elaine: Putonghua tutor. He tells me I have a very good ear for accents, especially for -

Rebecca: Right. Good.

Elaine: Where's Amah?

Rebecca checks her mobile.

Rebecca: This one's filling in Apparently.

Elaine: Is she

Rebecca: Next of kin? Illegal by way of ferryboat? Forty-third descendent of Confucius? No clue, could care less, long as she cleans this place up and, and *why* can't I hear anything?

Elaine: Double-glazed windows?

Rebecca: They couldn't *possibly* have been on break this whole time?

Hammering.

Fanny: Dey make much noisey-ah!

Rebecca: Whole place is falling apart!

Hammering stops.

Fanny: (In Cantonese.) You can't speak Chinese? That's messed up.

Elaine: Who's your contractor?

Rebecca: Secretary in the office recommended him. His name's Wing Wing or something.

Elaine: That was your first mistake Rebecca. *Never* trust a local.

Rebecca: Thought it was me. You know, "Gwei Los" can't be choosers?

Elaine: You're almost "one of us".

Rebecca: Yeah, you the local, me the "mixed bag". We're a couple heathens us.

Elaine: Let me talk to him. "Local-to-local."

Rebecca: For the record: you've been warned. (To Fanny.) Whatever your name is, can you get "Mr. Wing" out here?

Fanny: I finish cleaning here-ah but *still*

Rebecca: (To Fanny.) No, no I am not asking you to clean, I am asking you to bring Mr. Wing, the contractor out here please? (Slowly.) You go get him, man, the man in the bedroom. *M-goy saai*?

Pause.

Elaine: That you can recite Cantonese with such graceful fluency never ceases to amaze me.

Rebecca: Locals always seem remarkably nonplussed. Go-to-party-trick. You should see me pull it out during conference calls. The initial awe, shock and wonder for my lackluster yet keen grasp on the language, how because I look "really Chinese" I must therefore act, speak and assimilate Chinese. These remarks only made of course, after a few Tsing Dao's and the obligatory "my mother-in-law is a big fucking cunt" convo.

Elaine: Speaking of, shouldn't you be fluent by now?

Rebecca: Visit to Gran's in Sussex every Christmas. Without fail, "this is what England is really like" show! Half-breed Rebecca, half-born in the jungle must be reeducated as to the ways of the White man. Idle commentary on the weather, tea, custard creams, Kevin McCloud, binge drinking.

Elaine: This a "general observation" or "bitter recollection"?

Rebecca: Dad used to say I was one of the lucky few. Packed, stamped and shipped off to boarding school. "International schools are a fucking joke" he'd cry. Mum agreed with him too. Only thing they had in common.

Elaine: Lucky escape?

Rebecca: If you think boarding school's is a lucky escape, darling, then we've got *much* bigger problems

Elaine: Yes such as *where* on this godforsaken island can I find a good, decent, six-foot-two man with a freehold and an AAA rating? Strike that, long as he has dental, likes long walks on the beach I'm easy (beat.) Okay, let me see if I've got this right...

Pause.

Elaine: (In Mandarin.) Big man who make big noise in bedroom. Please eat him out for Mrs. Losey.

Fanny: WAH?

Elaine: That's about as far as we got I'm afraid. If you like I could get her to call and complain to the Water and Sanitation Department or

Rebecca: Its fine (beat.) You go and...go and clean the windows, alright?

Pause.

Rebecca: Windows. Over there.

Fanny: Win-doos?

Rebecca: "Win-doos" yes and use this.

Rebecca takes out window cleaner, hands it to her.

Fanny: Dis?

Rebecca: Use this. Like this.

Rebecca makes circular motions. Fanny points to the urn on the coffee table.

Fanny: Yes. I pick up dis.

Elaine is trying hard not to laugh.

Rebecca: (Rising.) Not that. The windows. Wash them. Wash the windows.

Fanny reluctantly goes to clean the windows.

Rebecca: How's trade?

Elaine: Oh. Same old (deadpan.) P&L's on the up and up.

Rebecca: *Wow.*

Elaine: I know

Rebecca: You need a holiday

Elaine: Putting all my bonuses towards buying my way *out* of that place.

Rebecca: You'd quit?

Elaine: Only became a broker

Rebecca: I always thought you'd teach

Elaine: Only became a broker because the general consensus was that I was only ever good for one thing out here in the "real world".

Rebecca: Which is?

Elaine: I'm a *great* talker.

Rebecca: (Laughs.) Joe used to call you "electric". Whatever that means. How you got us into those members only's "back in the day".

Elaine: I feel old.

Rebecca: Thirteen years

Elaine: Take a look at us now, eh?

Rebecca: Couple FILTH's.

Elaine: Come on, not *that* bad. Haven't set foot in Lan Kwai Since the handover.

Rebecca: I bet.

Elaine: Cross my heart.

Rebecca: Rescue me from a banal existence Elaine!

Elaine: You *love* it here.

Rebecca begins rooting around the pantry, putting away food when a cupboard door falls off its hinges and falls to the ground.

Rebecca: What am I going to *do* Elaine?

Elaine: We'll sort it out. *I'll* sort it out. Watch, when Mr. "Wingy" waltzes out here I'll tell him to go shove this half-assed renovation up his

Rebecca: No I meant...shit, time?

Elaine: Plenty of time

Rebecca: Sorry.

Rebecca takes out two cups.

Elaine: Took the day. What else am I here for if *not* to be brutally taken advantage of?

Rebecca takes out a bottle of whisky, holds it over one cup.

Elaine: Bit early for me thanks.

Rebecca pours whisky into her own, downs it.

Rebecca: Ricky mentioned he might stop by.

Elaine: Tonight?

Rebecca: Maybe.

Elaine: *Pissed* no doubt

Rebecca: Fingers crossed!

Elaine: If *only* he had put as much effort into staying politically-neutral in print, pubs, radio, reality as he did in sucker-punching that LCP.

Rebecca: LCP?

Elaine: Little Chinese Puppet. Also known as "Fong". Also known as gazillion dollar deal planned, propelled and put into action by yours truly only to be blown to bits and pieces by a pothead with a bigger ego than - *how* you put up with his hankering after approval, his incapability of seeing anything through, his inherent need to piss me off....

Rebecca: He was only defending me, my "honour" so-to-speak.

Elaine: How did he "defend" your honour exactly? By putting your career in jeopardy? I'm not saying – that man, mainlander, puppet, whatever, what he said to you at your Dad's funeral was totally utterly completely out of line but come *on*, he's investing over fifty mill.

Elaine's mobile beeps.

Rebecca: You don't think I know that? May not have been around the block as many times as you but I'm trying my -

Elaine: One second.

Elaine answers it.

Elaine: Wai? Oh hello! (Whispers.) Fong.

Pause.

Elaine: Yes that's, that's right, at that address. Of course! he wouldn't, no he's not. No problem. Yes.

Rebecca: Who on earth would *he* bring?

Elaine: Politically-incorrect Chinamen. Gotta love 'em with their bad breath and bullet wounds

Rebecca: Long as he's set to invest I couldn't give a toss what his breath smells like

Elaine: You're *welcome*.

Rebecca: Haven't I thanked you enough? Ugh! Forget I said that. This job!

Elaine: What, being editor-in-chief of the "top" English newspaper in Hong Kong not enough of a challenge?

Rebecca: PR's plugging the latest investment scheme, the opening of yet another "Louis Vuitton" on the corner of a heritage site in Central. One after the other after the other after the other

Elaine: You've had a lot to deal /with these last couple months

Rebecca: *That* is what being "editor-in-chief of the top English newspaper in Hong Kong" is all about. That is what being the sole surviving heir to a once-celebrated, once-syndicated, now staid, now penniless publication is all about. Guanxi rules!

Elaine: Your dad -

Rebecca: Know what you're going to say, *don't*

Elaine: I was *going* to say we never got to catch up properly... at the funeral

Rebecca: Had my hands full didn't I?

Elaine: You certainly did

Rebecca: What's *that* supposed to mean?

Elaine: Nothing. There you were, "in your element".

Rebecca: I'm not much fun these days, eh?

Elaine: No you're just-

Rebecca: Just?

Elaine: Lately, you've been a bit

Rebecca: Do I come across as withdrawn?

Elaine: Only meant...

Rebecca: (Rising.) High-strung? Incapable of orgasms? Reproductively challenged? What do the socialites, real-estate moguls and Tai Tai's of this little ole island think about me, really? Go on. You can tell me. Trying to garner a reputation in this town, tough gig for a woman.

Elaine: *Jesus* Rebecca! Nobody tells me anything.

Rebecca: Once you're good and past the child-bearing age bracket of twenty-five to thirty, reach a decent point in your career where you hold no more than a modicum of power and then...*boom*! On your way out, evicted, expelled, retired at sixty, no use to anyone and-

Elaine: You spend far too much time worrying about what other people think.

Rebecca: I'm not like you. You don't ever need to "try".

Elaine: I try. I try too hard. Do you miss London?

Rebecca: Sometimes

Elaine: We were a bit, bit wild weren't we? Ricks was the worst though. Schemer.

Rebecca: I was the odd Eurasian out.

Elaine: Designated driver.

Rebecca: Hair-holder.

Elaine: Divine prophet. Sophist. Guru.

Rebecca: *Boring*

Elaine: Night before we left. Up on the roof.

Rebecca: Bad idea

Elaine: Breaking in, getting caught. Worth it, cause once you got up there you could see everything, see the whole thing. We owned that city (beat.) Don't you find yourself wondering why, if we had it so good, why leave in the first place?

Rebecca: (Shrugs.) Joe.

Elaine: You had the privilege of belonging to both. I feel like somehow I feel like...I got away with it.

Rebecca: How do you mean?

Elaine picks up the pill bottle.

Elaine: Prozac?

Rebecca: Those aren't mine.

Fanny: Mista Loo-zee!

Elaine: Whose are they then?

Rebecca: What did you say?

Fanny: Come back jaast now.

Rebecca: *When* did he

Fanny: You have Mista Loo-zee for partay. Not so sad no more?

Rebecca: Sad? Whoever said I was/sad

Elaine: Joe's back/from

Rebecca: Yes he's back/back from, from -

Fanny: He no want/lunch. You want lunch?

Rebecca: I'm not hungry! Elaine, do you want?

Elaine: Wouldn't say no to a cuppa.

Rebecca begins making tea.

Fanny: I made good dinna tonight. Chicken fried wice. You
                love chicken fried *wice*, hah?

Rebecca: We've hired a caterer.

Fanny: Wah? Wah is "cater"?

Rebecca: We'll only need you to help with the, the clearing up,
                you know? That's *all*.

Fanny: No dinna?

Rebecca: No dinner. *Dishes.*

Fanny: I no understand!

Rebecca: "Jing-gon-zheng lah. M-ho-joy-fan leng?"

Fanny: (Confused.) Leng-ah?

Rebecca: Yes, uh, Leng! Leng..zai...?

Fanny: Ah! OK, OK. Ah Fung, he play wif Leng, wif Hitla!

Rebecca: Hitler?

Fanny: Naughty boy *dat* Hitla!

Elaine: Isn't he adopted?

Rebecca: *I* wouldn't know.

Joe enters.

Elaine: By those two gay bankers *whatstheirfaces*. I know! We
                should have the wake over at *their* place!

Joe: Sounds like a marvellous idea.

Elaine: Joe. Hullo!

Joe: There's a half-naked man in my bedroom.

Elaine: Heard you'd been...away. How *are* you?

Joe gives Elaine a peck on the cheek.

Joe: I'm OK and yes I was away, for a bit.

Elaine: Contractor.

Joe: Contractor?

Elaine: Shirtless bloke. Does he happen to be carrying a drill?

Joe: As it happens

Elaine: Kettle's boiled

Joe: "Boiling" today.

Elaine: Hundred degrees with a sprinkling of ninety-eight percent humidity.

Joe: Pollution *gazillion*.

Elaine and Joe laugh.

Joe: Still "cutting keyboards" Elaine?

Elaine: And calling strangers I've never met *big boy* so I can feel all *"self-important"*.

Joe: You never change

Elaine: Aw, shucks!

Joe: Rebecca has though. When?

Rebecca: When?

Joe: Your hair?

Elaine: Who'da thought Becca could pull off being a blonde?

Joe: *I* didn't.

Joe: I quite fancy a beer, if you *don't* mind.

Rebecca throws out the beer on the counter. She goes to the fridge, takes out another one - remains silent.

Joe: Only had the one. Hardly one. Half of one.

She hands him the beer.

Rebecca: You didn't say you'd be back.

Joe: "Surprise!"

Elaine: Everyone was asking /after you -

Rebecca: Such a shame we couldn't hold the service at your convenience

Joseph.

Joe: Better late than never.

Fanny begins moving Joe's bags.

Rebecca: (Rising.) Don't take those in yet *please*

Fanny: Baat Mista Loo-zey's bags?

Rebecca: Leave them there *please*.

Joe: You've a plan for me after all?

Fanny: You sure-ah you no want something to eat?

Rebecca: We're all fine, *really*. Go and clear off the coffee table. Clean. Table. Thank you!

Rebecca points to the bag on the coffee table, then begins taking off the covers from the furniture, a bit too forcefully.

Joe: Sorry about your Dad.

Rebecca: Why? He *hated* you.

Pause.

Joe: Couldn't have scheduled it any better myself, a vigil for the "pioneering figure of democracy" coinciding with the celebration of a decade of de-escalating democracy

Rebecca: Yeah, well, you know better than anyone how much my father *loved* irony!

Joe: Ricks coming?

Rebecca: Considering he socked one of most powerful businessmen on the planet in the face

Joe: Wait, what?

Elaine: At the funeral/he -

Joe blocks Rebecca's way around the sofa.

Rebecca: Why are you, oh would you move-out-of-the-way-please?

Joe: What's going on?

Rebecca: *Move*

Joe: One simple question Rebecca

Rebecca: *I am going to sack Ricky Forrester.*

Joe steps out of the way.

Joe: Only job he's ever had, only thing he's ever loved

Rebecca: Forrester "in love"? Oh forgive me, I had no *idea*, who knew there'd be room inside that poorly misshapen heavily-medicated heart?

Joe: He won't recover.

Rebecca: Richard Forrester will find another job!

Joe: Ricky Forrester, who lives in a squat on an outlying island, takes recreational drugs and entertains delusions of grandeur that he might someday be bestowed with the ability to beerpong whilst

> simultaneously standing on his head? He'll kill himself over the classifieds!

Rebecca is now ripping the sheets off the furniture...

Rebecca: Since your concern for him has returned all of a sudden why not put him in one of your pinstripe suits? Strap him to a Danish desk chair, get him imputing outputting numbers day in, day out, day in, day out whilst snorting what dignity you've got left cause that's all you do isn't it?

Joe: Have you thought about what I asked, before?

Rebecca: Haven't had time. All this.

Riiiipppp...

Joe: We could you know. Leave. Today.

Rebecca: Only *you* would on a day on *this* day.

Riiiipppp...

Joe: But?

She tears a sofa cushion.

Rebecca: Lovely!

Joe: Fixable.

Rebecca: Is it?

Lights in the flat go out.

Rebecca: No, SERIOUSLY?

Fanny turns on her mobile - she continually turns it on to create light.

Lights go back on.

Joe: There. All better.

Elaine: Rebecca? I best get a move on, get the rest of the -

Joe: What happened?

Rebecca: Happened? What "happened"? What happened was I lived, continued to live, to live *here* without you breathing down my neck blaming me for everything!

Elaine: I /should

Joe: I'm not blaming you

Rebecca: You leaving. Cry for help? Grand gesture? Grand demonstration of...I don't know, idiocy? Cause that's what you are, you're an idiot if you think you can come back here after months and months without – Take a look around Joe, take a good hard look. This is how *you've* lived for over a decade. Maid, chauffeur, home cooked meals, clean house every day, do you think you could go back?

Joe: Was home at least.

Rebecca: You wanted this.

Joe: Changed my mind. Guess I realized I'm not particularly good at being an expat.

Rebecca: So there's a few parties, a few evenings of painless schmoozing. Get over it, yourself! And FYI, unlike that "politically-correct psuedo-intellectual" who sent me halfway across the world to facilitate his dick I've made something out of myself (beat.) My father. Editor-in-chief. Honorary whore-monger Robert Hunter. Pillar of Hong Kong society, the "colonialist with a conscience", may he rest in peace. OK yes, in a past life he was a pioneering journo, you know, before his dipso "breakdown" into that pathetic guilt-ridden existence though we all know it was his ego that got the Enquirer into so much debt. He wasn't even capable of sustaining a part-time job lecturing housewives, let alone his underage "girlfriends" he insisted on keeping locked away with their disposable incomes and whitening creams!

Elaine: Got to...

Joe: He was a good man

Elaine: Got to go and

Joe: You're more in demand than ever. You revel in this new life whilst I...the day I left you, wait, *don't* turn away from me I want, I *need* to tell you this. One of those long days, you have them, we all have them but this day, longest fucking day of my entire fucking life of doing nothing, absolutely *nothing* and I -

Rebecca claps - clap clap clap.

Rebecca: *You* had a "long day"? *You* had the "longest day of your life"? Well congratu-fucking-lations Joseph. You get the special prize. Buy one, get nothing free!

Joe: What's so funny?

Rebecca: Not laughing.

Joe: What's so funny about not wanting to wake up in the morning?

Rebecca: What these are for I suppose?

She picks up the pill bottle.

Joe: Don't you see? Why can't you see? Tell me to be still. Tell me we can go home (beat.) together.

Rebecca: I *am* home.

Joe: You're not even going to consider.

Rebecca: Not leaving.

Joe: Something you should know.

Rebecca: About?

Joe: About

Rebecca: Can't deal with it, you, right now!

Joe: Can't wait!

Joe grabs her.

Rebecca: *Getoffme!*

Joe: That's it!

Rebecca: What's *"it"*?

Fanny: Missus Loo-zee where you want dis-ah?

Joe: Job's over, done with –

Rebecca: You quit?

Fanny: Where dis go-ah?

Fanny attempts to lift the basket holding urn, fails.

Joe: No, fired!

Fanny: Vewy heavy.

Rebecca: Of *course* you were!

Fanny accidentally drops the basket with the urn onto the ground, it makes a loud thump, tips out...ashes everywhere..

Fanny: Sowwy sowwy!

Joe: Yeah. Right there. Good place for him.

Rebecca: CAN'T YOU DO ANYTHING RIGHT?

Fanny retrieves the vacuum cleaner -she is just about to vacuum the ashes...

Rebecca: STOP! Stop...moving. Elaine...?

Rebecca motions to Elaine who quickly grabs the vacuum away from Fanny.

Rebecca: Remind me the to use this uppity prepubescent again. I mean, hello, "Hello-Kitty"!

Joe: Not her fault you're being such a...

Rebecca: Go on. Go on. No holds barred, naked, in-all-sincerity truth, what the hell am I, Joe?

She grabs the pill bottle off the table, throws it at him. The bottle breaks open, pills spill out onto the floor.

Rebecca: Who the hell are you? Do you even know what you've become? Do you?

Joe: Hell hath no limits, where hell is, there must we ever be.

Fanny begins picking pill after pill from off from the floor.

Rebecca: This isn't fucking Faust Joe! This is life, real life.

Joe: Tell me the truth and I'll go.

Rebecca: Where will you go? No, don't answer that, not-my-problem. Oh remember to get yourself tested for Chlamydia, hear its going round the stripper circuit, see it tends to make women infertile!

Joe: You've nothing else to say to me?

Rebecca: (Quietly.) Where were you?

Joe: Funny the way in which clarity comes. For me it was tiles moving across a board, blaring Bloomberg screens. Deafening sounds of a city. Never (beat.) ending. Passing an open door, a stream of light through a keyhole. Not belonging. I love you Rebecca, I just wish you wouldn't make everything so fucking complicated!

Joe exits.

Fanny: (In Cantonese.) Is the air-conditioner broken?

Rebecca: Everyone's left!

Elaine: I'm here. I've always been here.

Rebecca puts the urn back on the coffee table.

Fanny: (In Cantonese.) Yep. The air-conditioner is definitely broken.

Rebecca goes to the kitchen, pours herself another drink.

Elaine: Haven't you had enough?

She downs one after the other...

Elaine: Don't you think Joe's a little bit right about -

Rebecca: Either join the party Elaine or *get out*.

Elaine: Nothing I do or say right now will make a difference.

Rebecca: But isn't that what we do, what we expats do, "make a difference?"

Pause.

Elaine: I'll call you.

Elaine exits.

Fanny: (In Cantonese.) What is "Chlamydia"?

Rebecca: Nobody gets out of here alive!

Lights in the flat go out.

Rebecca: One shouldn't drink alone or in the semi-dark. Hey, you, hello, Hello Kitty? Would you like one? No? Fine. Suit yourself.

She pours out the rest of the bottle.

Rebecca: To sully this goose would do me a great honour. Chin chin.

She downs it. Lights go back on.

Fanny: (In Cantonese.) You people drink *a lot.*

Rebecca: I heard that.

Fanny: Missus Loo-zee?

Rebecca: Maybe if I close my eyes

Pause.

Rebecca: Let's make a toast. To my father here and to control!

Lights go back on.

Rebecca, growing steadily drunk -

Rebecca: Been putting a lot into perspective lately. Yeah. Getting through a single day, bloody hard but I *have* to put things into perspective!

She pours herself another one.

Fanny: (In Cantonese.) You have some serious "Daddy issues".

Rebecca: What? Oh I don't know. He'll go to Ricky's probably. He'll probably *probably* be a sobbing sweaty mess right now. Hope he is a wet whimpering sobbing sweaty...what was I saying? – I can't stop, my mind that is. I'm moving so fast that if I stop I'll never be able to start up again. Routine is my punishment – Funerals. Bloody funerals – Kitty? Kitty, how well did you know your father? You don't have to answer that. None of my business. But I don't recall having a single conversation with mine lasting more than ten minutes. When he did...let me set the scene for you, Kitty. As he steps over the littered carcasses of the half-wits, those who dare-to-challenge the then slowly imploding media empire, poor buggers, he would then turn his head towards me, ever so slowly, power play you see and every time he'd ask the same thing (beat.) How's the marriage Rebecca, the inability to conceive children? Send my assistant a memo, your birthday, you know I *always* forget. You failed Rebecca. You failed me and I owe you nothing. Failed to find yourself a proper partner, proper vocation, reason for being, failed to continue the line, my line, the "Hunter lineage" and, and you're a...

Rebecca: Nobody wants to take the time to get to know me, to get to know the real me. Joe, Elaine, Ricks. Even you. You must think, *what* you must think (beat.) Time. Time's this far off thing I can't reach it. In control, out of control. I'm on this cliff and when I look down all I see are my mistakes. So I don't. I don't ever look down. I don't ever look back.

Fanny: You want me wash wind-oos? OK?

Rebecca: I'm going out! Right out. Mm. You're right though I *should* change first.

Rebecca begins undressing - Fanny looks on in horror.

Rebecca: Look a right state, wrong shoes. Ha! Black, slimming but fucking depressing! (Laughs.) You, uh, you stay here Kitty, keep Dad company he'll like you, he'll really...you stay and and and do whatever it is...whatever it is you do.

Rebecca exits.

End of Act I

46

Act 2

Revolutions

Later. Ricky Forrester's bungalow - Lamma Island.

Open plan kitchen living room. There are unwashed dishes in the sink, dirty laundry litters the floor, Chinese and Australian paraphernalia fill the flat, perhaps a small standing fan whirring away somewhere. Large bust of Chairman Mao in one corner. Under the coffee table - a stack of old stained copies of the Hong Kong Enquirer. Sliding doors lead to an outdoor patio.

Ricky [clad only in silk robe] is fast asleep on the grotty sofa. Dozen or so beer cans are left on the table, one is balanced on his bare stomach. There is a large bruise on his left cheek.

Lights up on Joe who is standing over Ricky. He moves over to the window, tripping over a few beer cans. Ricky stirs, opens his eyes, stretches, the beer can falls from his stomach, rolls to the floor at Joe's feet.

Ricky, half-asleep -

Ricky: Mind the Fosters mate (beat.) how are you going?

Joe: Fine, as fine as anyone can be after a twelve hour flight with little to no sleep followed by a bitch-fight with the wife and *Jesus* Ricky, what happened to your face?

Ricky: Joe?

Joe: Does it hurt much?

Ricky: Much?

Joe: Looks *awful.*

Ricky: Joey?

Joe: Yes?

Ricky: Joe what, what are you *doing* here and how did you get *in*?

Joe: You did say, "door is always open"!

Ricky straightens up, picks up a beer can off the floor, tips it over, it's empty - not good.

Ricky: I, I don't remember...

Joe: Sure you do. Midnight, "Mad Dogs" down in Wanchai for my thirtieth? You treated all us middle aged "yobs" to Jager shots.

Ricky: I did?

Joe: Back when you were peddling low class, Grade B drugs to triads. Poor punters.

Ricky: Oh right. Good, good times. Shouldn't you be, like, I dunno, home?

Joe: Don't tell me you and your, your "used beer bongs" were busy?

Ricky: Does your "wife" know? Be a dearie Joey, pass us a durrie.

Ricky points at the carton of cigarettes on the other side of the room. Joe throws it to him.

Ricky: *M-goi-saai*! Now, where'd I put my...

Ricky rises - his robe loosens - opens - reveals everything.

Joe: *Fucksake*

Ricky: Nothing you ain't seen before Joey.

Ricky re-ties his robe. He falls to his knees and begins rifling through the stacks of papers under the coffee table.

Joe: What are you *doing*?

Ricky begins throwing magazines and rubbish out from under it.

Ricky: Bic.

Joe: Bic?

Ricky: Here Biccie. Here Bic. Bic Bic Bic Bic...

Joe: Why'd you live all the way out here anyway?

Ricky: Aside from the fact it costs chips, think the locals will be livid if I abandoned ship and I happen to *like* it d'you mind?

Joe: Nobody "likes" living in fucking Mordor next to fucking Groucho Marx and is that, is that a bust of Chairman Mao?

Ricky: You admiring my handiwork?

Joe: You sculpt now?

Ricky: Steal, occasionally

Joe: All part of "what-people-will-think" protocol?

Ricky: Ha-ha. You're such a dag

Joe: You never finished

Ricky: *Always* finish mate

Joe: Finished *telling* me how you got that big blue purple epic thing on your face

Ricky: Don't worry your pretty big head about it.

Ricky finds a bag full of pot, takes a big whiff.

Ricky: Not bad. *There* you are my pretty...

Ricky finds his "bic" (lighter), lights up under the table. He exhales deeply.

Ricky: When'd you get here?

Joe: Am I enough of a cliché for you? Headlines read: "Coked-up banker abandons family, seeks refuge in the arms of Australian philosopher on outlying island."

Ricky: Too bloody early!

Joe: For?

Ricky: You. This. Whatever "this is". Though it's *awfully* nice of you to pop by after...how long's it been, a whole flipping year or summat?

Joe: More like three months and, and I apologized!

Ricky: You were always pretty crap at apologies Joey

Joe: You don't look as sharp when you're being smug

Ricky: How do I look the rest of the time?

Pause.

Joe: Can I bum one?

Ricky hands him the joint. Joe takes a hit, begins coughing.

Ricky: Shit's strong, eh? Got it off an ex-missionary in Ma On Shan.

They pass the joint back and forth.

Joe: Never be *quite* good enough for her.

Ricky: Rebecca's merriment lies in manufacturing misery for the modern man!

Joe: You've always had a way with words

Ricky: I *am* a writer.

Joe: *Exactly.* (beat.) *Why* I came back here!

Ricky: No clue *why* either but you can stay. Welcome to the ghetto!

Joe: Where do I go?

Ricky: I'm in there. You're out here.

Joe: Why do *you* get the -

Ricky: Cause *I* was here first. Neh-neh-neh-neh-neh.

Joe: Man-child

Ricky: All grown up

Joe: *You* clearly haven't

Ricky: Nice...deflecting is it?

Joe: "Projecting" and I wasn't, I was merely clarifying your...what *is* this exactly?

Ricky: What's what?

Joe: "Pilgrimage" sans "soul searching". How long's it been?

Ricky: One word for you mate. Freedom.

Joe: *Hungry*

Ricky: Don't have anything.

Joe: You don't have *anything*?

Ricky: Not unless you think a can of baked beans and a bag of kettle chips equates to proper nourishment. Might have some hummus left or gin (beat.) No gin, sorry!

Joe: I see

Ricky: You do, you see "the real" me?

Joe: Rebecca's dad would say

Ricky: "Cunt"?

Joe: Richard Forrester, Australian expatriate suffering from mid-life *crises*. Slumming clubbing snorting and soaking it up in Hong Kong *probably* after being banished from every other South East Asian city within the borders of the Golden Triangle. Hong

Kong was the only one left *other* than Chiang Mai of course. You don't have to be a genius to work it out just watch "The Beach"!

Ricky: Name's "Ricky" mate and

Joe: And he'd say "you're a slob" *mate*

Ricky: May be a *bit* but that's part of its charm. You'll soon get used to it. Can't afford a maid, unlike *some*.

Joe picks up a flyer from the floor -its a funeral programme.

Joe: Big turnout?

Ricky: Anybody whose anybody was there

Joe: Her old man got me this job. My first, only and last job.

Ricky: What/ what?

Joe: (Sings.) But what can a poor boy do? Except sing for a rock 'n' roll band?

Ricky: (Sings.) Cause in sleepy London town there's just no place for a

In unison:

Ricky: Street fighting man!

Joe: Street fighting man!

Ricky: Do I astound you?

Joe: You astound...

Ricky stops shorts - grabs his knees in pain.

Ricky: Argh.

Joe: Me.

Ricky: Argh!

Joe: You OK there?

Ricky: Bloody knees!

Joe: Ah, to be twenty-three. You, me, Stolichnaya and the "Street Fighting Man".

Ricky: Classic for a reason mate.

Joe: D'you have your HSBC on you?

Ricky: My *what* mate?

Joe: Your "Dieu et Mon Droit" mate.

Ricky roots through his pockets, takes out cash, bank card, coins.

Ricky: Tenner do the trick?

Joe shakes his head, snatches up Ricky's bank card then extracts a twenty pound note from his own pocket. He kisses it.

Joe: Queenie's the only girl for me.

Joe expertly rolls the note. He takes out a small packet of coke and begins cutting the powder with the bank card.

Ricky: (Laughs.) Never thought I'd live to see the day. *You* having a dealer on speed dial!

Joe: Don't you bloody well judge -

Ricky: I've *never* judged you Joey but since when -

Joe snorts a line.

Joe: Same as you Ricks, same as you. Boredom. Plain and simple fucking boredom!

Ricky: I am many things Joey but I ain't bored

Joe: You think I sound ungrateful.

Ricky: I don't think anymore. Gets me into trouble

Joe: How you got "the face"?

Ricky: Word wanker may have been uttered, albeit inappropriately.

Joe: Oh Ricky, tut-tut!

Ricky: Oh Joey, save it for the rest of the "Sycophants sporting Saville Row"!

Joe: Gladly, if I still or ever was a "Sycophant sporting Saville Row".

Ricky: You're not

Joe: No longer

Ricky: You mean

Joe: Redundant, fired, whatever. Lets not go into it. Lets get back to how you got your face/fucked up

Ricky: No, no don't change the subject. Which one was it?

Joe: I fired (beat.) myself. So to speak.

Ricky: You told Rebecca the "good news"?

Joe: What do *you* think?

Ricky: She told me you told her, you were going away for a week or...or something.

Joe: *When* did she

Ricky: Oh you know. Checking up on her and stuff. For you.

Joe: Right

Ricky: You never reply to any of my bloody e-mails!

Joe: Had a lot to think about

Ricky: Man with the perfect life, perfect everything spends more time "in pursuit of"?

Joe: Not perfect

Ricky: Outside looking in

Joe: Whenever I say, said those words "I'm a Banker", "Analyst", there was this moment. Disbelief then disgust for -

Ricky: For the intense innate fear, anger and loathing for it?

Joe: Anywhere else on the planet you're a fucking leper. Here in Honkers though? Badge of honour!

Ricky: Why'd you bloody well do it then?

Joe: End up like you? No job no girl no hope?

Ricky feigns being shot in the stomach, falls to the floor.

Ricky: Oof! Hitting the mark today Joey. Besides, I'm a changed man

Joe: She's changed too

Ricky: Who?

Joe: Changed her hair

Ricky: Oh yeah. She's a "bona fide blonde" now

Joe: *What* a statement. Passive. Superior. Bitch.

Ricky: Not fair

Joe: All's fair in love and a good fuck!

Ricky: Joey lets not do this, *that* right now. I got a thing later, ya know? So lets...get whatever, air, booze, food, alright? Be good for you. Be good for me.

Joe snorts another.

Joe: Liking this fine.

Ricky: Gotta take your, my, our mind off everything!

Joe: How?

Ricky: Maybe experience a little more of the culture around here?

Joe: Sub-culture, you mean

Ricky: Lamma Island welcomes "degenerates and dog-eaters"!

Joe: Left my -

Ricky: Borrow whatever you like mate. *What?*

Joe picks up a Hawaiian printed shirt off the floor.

Joe: For your own and mankind's sake, burn this.

Ricky: This here's a collectible mate. Circa '97. It's...it's vintage!

Joe: You forget Ricky everything here is at least two decades behind.

Ricky: Sold me on it. What a great businessman you are Joe Joe.

Ricky throws the old shirt away, puts on the shirt, pulls on a pair of trousers.

Ricky feigns being shot in the stomach, falls to the floor.

Joe: Beginning it meant nothing. Clients. Obligation. Etiquette. A way to "close the deal". Bit of fun. Cheap thrills. Drugs a given. Girls a given. They were doing their jobs too. Grinding against bloated equity traders pays the bills for their three-hundred-square-foot hole-in-the-wall studios and new getups for the next striptease. Weekend before I left. You covered for me

Ricky: *Your* excuse.

Joe: I came back didn't I?

Ricky: *Your* alibi.

Joe: We'd hooked up with a couple investment bankers. Their "first trip to the orient". Said they were going to show us how they did, drink hard, play hard "Square Mile style". Kept calling me "boy." Everything was "Boy, yeah boy. Yeah boy you never had it so good." – Back in London the market looked one big fucking graphic green, grey and orange Bloomberg TV tragedy. A "foreshadowing like no other"! For them, a week-long bender in Hong Kong littered with logistics and lap dancers was a godsend.

Ricky: You know such *lovely* people Joey.

Joe: Booked into a hotel. Pretty buzzed. Friday's delivery was late, boys start getting agitated, pacing, back forth, back and forth, can you imagine? Bunch of spoilt, Toff prigs prancing about, jumping onto gilded diamond-encrusted beds chanting all-in-unison to The Stone Roses? They couldn't clock my accent though, couldn't figure out who I was, that I was, that I was one of them.

Ricky: Yeah I noticed you starting to sound like a right flat Yank

Joe: Tailor-made pronunciation for the global citizen Richard. You flatten in order to flatter, facilitate.

Ricky: Before I dropped out, our exodus weekend jaunt to Brighton, just you and me. Remember? Your Mum spent the whole time telling me how hard you practiced being "posh-like". What a woman your Mum. Give her my regards?

Joe: I did

Ricky: How long, before

Joe: Before she found out that I was yet again taking advantage of her maternal hospitality, keeping up the pretense that I was loved-up, successful, happy? Eventually. Spent the night in the station. Nothing like sleeping on a piss-soaked bench whilst a drunk homeless man jerks off on you. I suggest you try it.

Ricky: Where'd you go from there?

Joe: Dad's. D'you know he moved to the middle of fucking Midlands?

Ricky: Bet he was thrilled-

Joe: First thing he says to me after ten years: "Oh. how *very* profound". This followed by a shot of Jack and "How's Ricky Forrester doing these days"? He's still so in love with you.

Ricky: He loves the part I play. The lone "Boy from Oz most likely to end up face-down on a hemp carpet with his nose in a jar."

Joe: You've played it to the hilt

Ricky: Joey, you had your whole life mapped out for you. You had people, dad, mum, Rebecca, Elaine people believing in you. I wanted to be a different person. Meeting you, moving out here. Beautiful accident.

Joe: Die is cast.

Ricky: You understand I had to protect her Joey

Joe: Heard the whole sob story on the ferry ride here

Ricky: You did? Who from?

Joe: Who *didn't* I hear it from! You're the talk of the town Ricks. Even that, that Fag with the Thai houseboy who lives down the road, he says you have a mean right hook

Ricky: Hairdresser from Melbourne

Joe: Fisticuffs were deserved, were they? He insult a national Australian pastime or was his ugly "Maoist" mug gunning for punishment?

Ricky: Rebecca

Joe: Her name provokes the most parochial of men to commit violent acts!

Ricky: Saunters in *late*.

Joe: My kind of guy.

Joe cuts a new line of Coke.

Ricky: Followed by his "entourage". Bunch of morons who don't bother concealing their "Crackberries". Becca's reading from some poem...

Joe: "We sit late, watching the darkness unfold, no clock counts this." Recently departed Rob Hunter, he loved Ted Hughes. Please, continue.

Pause.

Ricky: She manages to finish, gracefully I thought considering the scene they were making. *What* a performance. Titter titter giggle gaggle. Disgusting. She makes her way back down the aisle, he stands, motions her to him.

Joe: Like this?

Joe makes a grand bowing gesture.

Ricky: Nah. More...

He clicks his fingers.

Joe: What was he?

Ricky: Receding hairline. Oh you meant, he's to be made (if he hasn't already) partner.

Joe: Partner-in-crime

Ricky: Pulled a fast one. Found out right before the funeral...from the bloody intern!

Joe: Had no idea the *Enquirer* was in so much trouble

Ricky: You didn't wanna

Joe: He give her a "stern-talking-to"?

Ricky: He touched her fucking tits! He was, he was feeling her, touching her, grabbing her body like it belonged to him like she was one of those porcelain Guanyin "Mercy" goddesses.Leaning in close, spit dribbling from his chin, she was straining backwards, shaking, struggling to, holding back from retaliating. I had to, I had to -

Joe: You lost it.

Ricky: I lose it. Tap him on the shoulder. "Private conversation" he says. I demand he apologize. Becca looks at me, daggers, "Have you lost your mind?" I tell her what I saw. What nobody else saw, but I saw it, "I saw him taking taking taking." She looks at the floor. Her eyes stay on the floor, "This is Ricky Forrester" she says. Receding hairline's eyes widen. He puts out a hand. I don't take it. He smiles, tells me its a real pleasure to meet the employee so notorious amongst his compatriots. Compatriots? Don't you mean repressed, misogynistic pieces of pond scum? He keeps his composure "I'm afraid Ricky, there's going to be some changes at the Enquirer." I call him a commie and pretty soon, bastard's bleeding all over the marble shrieking for retribution, my head on a stick. His muscle men run over, beat me to a bloody, Becca attempts to diffuse the situation, I try to make sense of it all. How can you work for that dick Rebecca how? She shrugs, stalks off, leaves me to the...and it *still* hurts, my ego more so than the left side of my face!

Joe: Is she OK?

Ricky: Oh she's alright but nobody fucking believes me!

Joe snorts another line.

Joe: Course nobody fucking believes you.

Ricky: You believe me though right?

Snort snort.

Ricky: Why'd you leave us, eh? I mean, not like you've been around much anyway for the past few years but this time, this time when she really needed you, when the only person in the world she had left was lying there. Hours days weeks not knowing whether he's gonna live or die, you weren't around when they were talking about radiating sterilizing him, you weren't standing there waiting watching his body his soul *burning* -

Joe: Shut up. SHUT UP!

Ricky: Ooh, nerve

Joe: You're not special

Ricky: Hope it was worth it

Joe: She reminded me of Rebecca. Not in the eyes. Not the same eyes.

Ricky: Who and what are we talking about here?

Joe: Her name was Angelique. I picked her up at a

club. She danced, we danced, chatted for a bit. Her English was...I needed a hit. She said she dealt in the finest finery, the best Coke I'd ever...best part is she brought me home! Really, I'm not kidding! I snuck back a bottle of champagne, she takes off all her clothes, shrugs on my (laughs.) This makes her feels special, "shiny, new". She does what I tell her. Everything's simpler. I do a line. I do another and another until I see her, until I see Rebecca, wife materialize before me and I take pleasure in watching her eyes well up whilst I declare her a good for nothing halfwit sexless childless bulimic idiot bitch *anything* I can think of that will stop me from coming down because coming down from that high...next morning I left.

Ricky: You wonder if it all comes down to having control over them

Joe: Them?

Ricky: Feelings and things. I think.

Joe: I regret

Ricky: Don't tell *me* that!

Joe: Well?

Ricky: Start by trying not to dwell on the many of your marital slipups

Joe: When was your last relationship Ricks? But of course! You've never actually *had* a relationship

Joe: Ha.

Ricky: What?

Joe: Ha!

Ricky: Fine, be that -

Joe: You fucked her!

Joe shoves Ricky, hard.

Ricky: Where the *hell* did that come from?

Joe: I'm a banker Ricks! Gotta always be on the ball, so let's get the ball rolling shall we? Did you or did you not sleep with my wife?

Ricky: How can you ask me, after -

Joe: Do not say you were "a shoulder to cry on".

Ricky: I was there for her as a friend. She needed someone!

Joe: She's got a maid, chauffeur, staff of a thousand, how could she possibly need you? Don't lie to me.

Ricky: Mate!

Joe: Did you fuck her? Did you -

Ricky: No I did *not* sleep with Rebecca, alright?

Joe: Alright. Oh and by the way, in case you hadn't realized, she chose me! So admit it!

Joe shoves Ricky.

Joe: Admit

Ricky: Hey! Get your -

Joe shoves him again.

Joe: ADMIT.

Ricky fends him off.

Ricky: Touch me again Joe I swear -

Joe: You'll what? Give me one? OK then. I'm ready, I'm willing. Give it to me! Give it to me, I deserve it. I DESERVE -

Ricky punches him. Joe falls to the floor.

Joe: Argh! Fuck fuck fuck.

Silence.

Ricky goes to the kitchen, gets out some ice from the fridge. He returns to the living room, rests the ice on Joe's face.

Joe: I hate my life

Ricky: Liar

Joe: I hate my life

Ricky: Liar

Joe: I'm sorry

Ricky: You're sorry

Joe: I never slept with the stripper!

Ricky: Okay

Joe: I slept with Elaine

Ricky: You slept with Elaine

Pause.

Joe: Yes

Pause.

Ricky: Before you left?

Joe: Yes. No. On. Off.

Ricky: (Sighs.) Do you even have a line Joey?

Joe: I have a line

Ricky: Seems to me, no line

Joe: We make the best liars don't we? Rebecca and

I? Made for each other. She despises me for not wanting more I hate her for not wanting me enough.

Ricky gives the ice to Joe.

Ricky: Swelling should go down in a couple hours.

Joe stands up, walks over the window, sees something, jerks away.

Joe: Shit

Ricky: What's wrong?

Joe: She's outside

Ricky: Who's outside?

Joe: Get rid of her?

Ricky: You *didn't*

Joe: Thought I gave her the slip

Ricky: Piece of work

Joe: Wait!

Ricky: I'm going to let her in. Prepare yourself.

After a short pause, Joe nods.

Ricky slides open the patio door, goes out. He returns followed by Elaine.

Elaine: (To Ricky.) What did you do?

Ricky: What did *I* do?

Elaine: Obviously.

Joe: Totes obvs *darling*.

Elaine: You punched him in the face!

Ricky: A hit, a palpable hit!

Joe:	He punched me in the face
Ricky:	Now that's settled. Gonna leave you two/to it
Joe:	Stay Ricks
Elaine:	What is this, some sort of "intervention"?
Ricky:	Some sort of bloody summat!
Joe:	Don't you miss the blissful monotony of university?
Ricky:	Uh, no.
Joe:	Lecture pub, pub lecture, pub, pub, lecture...
Elaine:	Rented tuxedos
Joe:	"Signet ring crew".
Elaine:	Dancing all night.
Joe:	Decent E
Ricky:	You were taller then
Joe:	Ooh, was I now?
Elaine:	What about me?
Joe:	You were the best looking blonde introvert I'd ever seen!
Ricky:	*Bored* now.

Ricky puts his arms around Elaine.

Elaine:	Careful with the merchandise. I may be worth billions next week.
Ricky:	Congrats Ellie
Joe:	What's this?
Elaine:	*Waiting*
Ricky:	I promise never again to call one of your potential

clients an "oppressive sadist who publicly supports the one-child-policy".

Elaine: Pond scum. You called Fong pond scum.

Ricky: (Sing-song.) And I gave that Fong Pond Scum a real good one

Elaine: That's mature

Ricky: I sorry lah

Ricky saunters up to Elaine.

Elaine: What're you up to Ricky Forrester?

Ricky suddenly grabs Elaine, begins tickling her. Joe looks on expressionless. Elaine moves out of Ricky's grip.

Elaine: (Laughs.) How old *are* you?

Ricky: Shouldn't ask a lady her age. Don't you want to sink to my level?

Joe: Surely this calls for a celebration, I mean "libation"?

Elaine: No. Coffee.

Elaine moves to the kitchen.

Ricky: She'll end up putting us all to shame

Joe: D'you think that's what she wants? Why don't we ask her? Elaine, at this very moment what do you want? You can have anything.

Elaine: Anything?

Joe: Anything

Ricky: Stiff drink, BBC Four, a good fuck and a big bed!

Joe: Was *asking* Elaine

Elaine still can't find the coffee.

Elaine: I have no idea. Where's your (beat.) What this place needs

Ricky: A woman's touch

Elaine: When are you going to let me redecorate?

Ricky: How's "never"? I prefer to keep recreation, self-actualization and renovation to a minimum thank you.

Elaine: Well you'll have more time on your hands now that (beat.) Ricky I'm

Ricky: You're awfully sorry but I've been cast out of the Garden of Eden! Yeah I figured that's why you graced my humble bungalow with your fair presence

Elaine: He's threatening to sue

Joe: Classic Rebecca. Sending you out here to do her dirty work

Ricky: She's dealing with stuff Joey. Anyway past is past, right?

Elaine: Right

Joe: You're taking this very well

Ricky: More important work to be done

*Ricky stands, puts on his jacket - there's a large pink badge with "**WE WANT UNIVERSAL SUFFRAGE HK 2007!**" printed on it. He then puts on a pink headband.*

Elaine: Politicos won't know what hit 'em.

Joe: Where the hell are you going dressed like that?

Elaine: Every year without fail, Forrester rallies for the Hong Kong people's right to vote.

Ricky: Come with? Biggest turnout since 2003

Joe: Innit.

Elaine: *Busy.* You may recall, post-funeral there's this thing where friends and family gather in a room to mourn the loss of a loved one?

Ricky: Half a million. Pounding the streets. Giving a shit.

Joe, in a cheesy "newsreader" voice:

Joe: Ricky Forrester, soon to be ex-editor of the *Enquirer* newspaper will march for the rights and freedoms of the Hong Kong people tonight, convinced he's got the whole city in his back-pocket. He knows what this city's in for. Tell us Ricky, what's it matter what you do? What does any of it matter? D'you think anyone gives a shit?

Ricky: I happen to give a shit

Joe: The hypocrisies of these people!

Ricky: *Here* we go...

Joe: The way they swill and spout their ideologies like they were God's gift to the people of this city, like they were bringing them something "new and improved, change for the better." They move here, *supposedly* for a new life but instead of actually *living* here, they just hole themselves up, leading insignificant half-lives in half-worlds, why not just build a ghetto, or a concession? Be hell of a lot easier!

Ricky: For who?

Joe: Barriers could be controlled by the consulates. Locals are allowed to take daily trips to these miniature enclosed states all for the reduced price of twenty Hong Kong "dollas"!

Ricky: (Deadpan.) Please, stop.

Joe: But before entering said-sanctimonious domain there'd be several prerequisites. Firstly, forget you are living in a foreign country, former colony. Really, fuck it. This is mini-Britain, mini-America, mini-Europe, there are no social classes, climbers, it never rains, there is no Queen, no Brummie accent, no Euro trash. Perhaps the occasional young unimpressed female parading around in her best designer footwear in search of a green card but in the end, only the "Gwei-Lo" remains. Forget people, forget culture. Chopsticks, banned outright but if you want a good night out, visits to the neon-signed-strip-tease joints are not only doable, but encouraged!

Elaine: You're angry because you don't fit in? Could've told you that from the start!

Joe: We've made no effort whatsoever to "fit in"!

Elaine: Would you rather be living here, on Lamma Island with Ricky and the rest of the hippie backpackers smoking spliffs and skinny dipping? No offence.

Ricky: None taken. You got me. Nutshell.

Joe: Difference is, he actually *likes* being the Hunter S. Thompson stereotype!

Ricky: Hang on

Elaine: This isn't *The Beach*

Joe: Every boy can dream!

Elaine: Listen to yourself. Why?

Joe: *Telling* you why

Elaine: Why did you bother coming back?

Joe: Mistake?

Elaine: For once in your life!

Joe: You think my marriage was a mistake?

Elaine: I never said.

Ricky: *Enough!* Out there. Real people with real -

Joe: We three, we're fucking tragic

Ricky: Stop! Fucking stop! Stop and shut up and make a choice!

Joe: Choice? What choice?

Ricky: Stay, go!

Joe: Oh *that* choice.

Ricky: So choose!

Ricky exits.

Elaine: He's right.

Joe: Must be nice up there on your pedestal, oh-so-pious. You fucked your best friend's husband behind her back.

Elaine: Please

Joe: Stop playing the "godly samaritan."

Elaine: Don't believe in God, or labels. But you like labels don't you? They make you feel safe.

Joe: All warm an' fuzzy. Fancy a pop?

Joe cuts a new line.

Elaine: I quit. You *know* that.

Joe: Suit yourself.

Joe does a line.

Joe: You used to be fun.

Elaine: You can be the biggest prick.

Joe: Today all I seem to be doing is apologizing! I'm sorry Elaine. I'm so sorry I asked you to partake in a little harmless line of fun that, by the way, you seemed pretty into when we were together, what, last month, week, yesterday? Fuck if I remember! I'm sorry I'm not good enough for you, for Rebecca, Ricky, my parents, sorry for my whole sad nonexistence!

Elaine: You call, I come running. Rebecca, your wife, my friend, my oldest friend she ceases to exist. While we were having our, our "fun" I criticized her, chastised her. Putting her down meant pretending with me, pretending those paychecks bonuses perks weren't the things turning you on that I was turning you on...I'm such a fool. That's right isn't it? I was one your many fools-on-the-side?

Joe: I'd go back.

Elaine: Can't go back. (beat.) How long did we...? Since New Year's? Rebecca spent months planning. Unreasonably humid for December. I'd come straight from work, hair matted to my forehead, my skin felt so hot (beat.) You smiled at me from across the room. I didn't recognize you at first. Was as if, as if we were strangers, two unattached strangers facing one another's futures. Possibilities. I couldn't handle you and your smile anymore, couldn't handle small-talk with the pretentious, privileged set that I was to join in with. Rebecca's plan for me, to join her up there. I ran. Wine glass in hand. Found myself in the carpark, hoisted myself up onto a railing. I felt a cool hand on my leg. You'd followed me, the man I couldn't recognize. The look on your face. In your eyes I was a divine saint, a madonna, the most beautiful thing in existence. I dropped the glass, it shattered. Beautiful sound. I went down to you, asked you for a light. You left and I thought-

Joe: You should stop.

Elaine: Stop?

Joe: Waiting. For me.

Elaine: Not everything is about you (beat.) I stopped.

Pause.

Elaine: I think I'm going to teach

Joe: Yes I remember you telling me

Elaine: You

Joe: I remember everything

Elaine: You remember everything

Joe: Yes I remember you telling me

Elaine: You

Joe: I remember everything

Elaine: You remember everything

Joe: You'd be terrific

Elaine: Thanks.

Joe: When? When will you

Elaine: Soon

Joe: Here?

Elaine: Here. Not here. I hope it's here.

Joe: What's your secret?

Elaine: Give 'em what they want. Simple really

Joe: Simple!

Joe laughs...then suddenly he begins hyperventilating.

Elaine: What's wrong?

Joe: My heart. It's beating very fast...too fast...

Elaine: Sit down. Breathe in, out.

Joe: I was...was...why, *what* I liked about us. Being pursued by you I felt...I...and I'm...I'm sorry, I'm so fucking sorry Elaine.

Elaine: In...out.

Pause.

Elaine: What you said, "the way they swill and spout their ideologies"? That's you, me, Ricky, that's us. The "Gwei-Los", the "Gwei-pours", the exiles

Joe: In-denials

Elaine: That too

Joe: Need to

Elaine: You *need* to go home

Joe: I can't

Elaine: You will

Joe: Why didn't I leave the firm sooner? Because! Because it was sharp, shiny, golden, reflective, full of rampant complex capitalists, making money, trading figures... that first day I stepped out of the lift onto the corridor I don't remember seeing much, too busy straightening myself up, trying to hide the coffee stains on my cuff. I remember the feeling. Electric. Unrestrained. Blaring out from all directions. On, off, on, off, flowing charts, rolling screens fuck, Reuters even appeared beautiful to me! I thought *this* could be my (beat.) I *was* I am a nobody but to get to this place, to receive a piece of platinum plastic like the rest of them, weekends in Bali, Koh Samui, Cebu, best of everything (beat.) CEO sat me down. I was so off my face, took a few for the nerves. He told me it was an interesting time for the market. He liked blonde women and golden retrievers, loathed Hong Kong but it paid for his charters to St. Kitts. There was a certificate from Harvard above his desk. His eyes were warm though and I felt safe. Then he told me he liked risks, saw a risk in me, that's why he was taking me on, aside from the fact he was a close personal friend of Rebecca's father. I was to be an analyst he said, report rumours to portfolio managers, "Part of the team sonnie boy"! Buy, sell, distill. In the end he said, you'll achieve, purge, purify and I don't know, I didn't know *anything*, sitting there in front of him, knees together, knuckles buried, ear bent, eyes wide, inhaling his cigar smoke felt like I was going to puke in his lap but then but *then* (beat.) He told me I'd make a fortune.

Elaine: What's a fortune?

Joe: How can we love something we know nothing about?

Elaine: I don't know

Joe: I love you Elaine

Elaine: Not in the way I want.

Joe: I deserve this?

Elaine: Joe...

Joe: Dance with me?

They begin dancing. After a moment or two Joe begins humming.

Elaine touches his face gently.

Elaine: He hit you pretty hard.

Joe: In his way Ricky is far more sensitive than I am.

Elaine: First day of the rest of our lives. D'you remember when they said that?

Joe: How wonderful it felt.

Elaine: A "new era".

Joe: I gave up things

Elaine: Could be worse

Joe: Giving away my collection of Neil Young LP's to make room for a walk-in closet?

Elaine: I believe one calls it "compromise".

Joe: My name is Joe and I am an addict.

Elaine: There'll be a time of stillness, time of mourning. Doubts put to rest, you'll say to yourself, this is for the best, I'm done, better now, restored. But that hole, that gaping hole in the pit of your stomach, deep in your gut, that wonderful feeling - lost. Opening that first million dollar bonus, those little blue pills you take to achieve a soaring high, the noise and the lights and the white dust that never seems to land that surrounds you that you give in to, wholly, fully. To recover, you're going to have to resist that low groaning voice on the other end of the line, insiting, more, yes, more more more. You will begin

79

to salivate at the sight of flickering fluorescent bulbs. You'll want it even more then.

Joe: Typical Gwei-lo.

Elaine: Don't recommend attempting to defend your "ghost" self though. Now, or ever.

Joe: She fits. We don't. We're not.

Elaine: You've been in Hong Kong too long

Joe: I love her and I fucked it up

Elaine: Fight for her.

Joe: Bully me into surrendering?

Elaine holds his hand.

Elaine: Here I am. Waving the white flag.

Joe walks over to the kitchen, turns on the tap, washes the Cocaine down the sink.

Joe: Be in love be in love be in love be in love...

Elaine: What's that?

Joe: Maybe if I say it over and over again it'll come true.

End of Act II

Act **3**

Relevations

Evening. Losey's flat.

Fanny has completely taken over the flat. There are takeaway boxes on the kitchen counter, sheets have been taken off most of the furniture...

Lights up on Fanny - dancing and singing along to the stereo on full-blast:

Fanny: HEY HEY YOU YOU! I DUN LIKE YOUR BOYFWEND! HEY HEY, YOU YOU I THINK YOU NEED A NEW WAN! HEY HEY YOU YOU! I CAN BE YOUR GIRLFWEND!

She jumps onto the coffee table - her "big moment" - Ah Fung enters with a very drunk Rebecca. Hitler follows behind.

Rebecca: Good to be home again! Oops!

Rebecca stumbles. Ah Fung helps her lean on him.

Ah Fung: (In Cantonese.) What are you doing up there?

Rebecca: Hello "Hello Kitty"!

Fanny: (In Cantonese.) Admiring the view?

Rebecca: Look at you, way up there! View from the top! Spiritus Mundi! Amazing! ABSOLUTELY -

Fanny climbs down.

Rebecca: Oh. Weird.

Fanny: (In Cantonese.) What's up with her?

Ah Fung: (In Cantonese.) What does it *look* like "girlfriend"? What happened here?

Fanny: (In Cantonese.) Um, the workmen? God, workmen! They're such slobs!

Ah Fung: (In Cantonese.) Turn that shit off!

Fanny turns off the music. She sees Hitler in the kitchen, he picks up a slice of her pizza.

Fanny: (In Cantonese.) What's that doing in here again? Oy, don't touch my "Meat Lover's"! THAT PIZZA IS MINE!

Ah Fung: (In Cantonese.) Give it a break.

Fanny lunges at Hitler who runs into the living room. He hides behind Rebecca.

Rebecca: (To Fanny.) Please give me the name of your plastic surgeon. He did a smashing job. Your boobs are...well, they're beautiful that's what they are.

Fanny: (In Cantonese.) What's she saying?

Ah Fung: (In Cantonese.) She was admiring your boob job.

Fanny: (In Cantonese.) Boob job? I haven't had a boob job!

Rebecca: Don't worry, won't tell a soul, I'm known to be discreet. Sssssshhhhhhhh...

Ah Fung: (In Cantonese.) What a mess. The wake's in an hour.

Fanny: (In Cantonese.) Wake? Wake? A funeral wake? Thought, party?

Rebecca: Sssshhhhhhhhhhhhhhhhhhhhh...

Ah Fung: (In Cantonese.) Party for some I suppose.

Rebecca: Ssssshhhhhhhhhhhhhhhh...

Fanny: (In Cantonese.) Dead guy in the vase?

She points to the urn.

Ah Fung: (In Cantonese.) Right. "Party for the dead guy in the vase". Little help here?

Fanny and Ah Fung attempt help Rebecca onto the sofa but she swots them away.

Ah Fung: Please Missus Loo-zee!

Rebecca: (Sharply.) Stop fussing Ah Fung! Stop fussing Fung Fung. Thank you my good man, my Fung my Ah Fung. Fung Fung. Old and reliable dad used to say. Drive me anywhere, anytime. I say the word (lowers voice.) I'm a cracking employer aren't I? You think I don't care, that I'm the same as the rest of those...who pay minimum wage stick you in a closet and think they're above it all. I care, I listen. I see you listen, listening in. Though let's face it Ah Fung, you'd screw anyone over for a buck and a smoke!

Ah Fung: Happy to help Missus Loo-zee

Rebecca: Forgot what happy feels like

Ah Fung: (In Cantonese.) Help me with her!

Fanny: (In Cantonese.) Do I *have* to?

Rebecca: "Happiness forgets". Who said that?

They help her onto the sofa.

Fanny: (In Cantonese.) Her breath smells rank!

Ah Fung: (In Cantonese.) She was drowning her sorrows in a bar for old expats. Forgot her keys, wallet...dignity.

In English -

Ah Fung: Don't drink and drive kids!

Fanny: (In Cantonese.) She's ridiculous!

Rebecca: Head. Hands. Arms. Legs. Feet. Let me *die*.

Ah Fung: Rest Missus Loo-zee.

Rebecca: You won't leave will you?

Ah Fung: *Rest* Missus.

Rebecca: Listen. Listen to me. Both of you! This whole thing, this "Editor-in-chief" thing, this wake thing, this death thing, these things were *thrust* upon me. Never asked for them. *I* wanted to be a, a cartographer! No that's not, what's the job when you help people? What I *do* for this paper. I *am* the bloody *Enquirer*! No what I meant to say is I'm, well *why* I'm like this why am I *this*? Whole life is...

Fanny: (In Cantonese.) Can she be anymore pathetic?

Ah Fung: (In Cantonese.) I feel sorry for the next generation

Fanny: (In Cantonese.) I *am* the next generation "old man".

Ah Fung: (In Cantonese.) Hey Fanny, guess how old I am.

Fanny: (In Cantonese.) Why?

Ah Fung: (In Cantonese.) Because it'll be fun

Rebecca: I present to you a "media empire" *restored*, where archaic, anarchic old men perpetuate puffed-up parasitic ideals to the public! Big pain in my arse. Did I ask for it? Please, please entrust me with handling a bureaucratic piss-hat paper devoid of any real opinion, which reads like a piece of fucking copy for a line of bespoke sustainable lamp shades made out of Caviar! What did you say? Eighty-nine hour work week handling mollycoddled brats who think they're all "just because" they went to Oxford and did work experience at *The SCMP*, *Time Out* and *Hong Kong Magazine*? Sign me up! (beat.) Dad's left, Joe's left. Step right up. Come on ladies and gents, step right up, whose next?

Fanny: (In Cantonese.) Does this mean I don't have to finish cleaning up?

Rebecca: Step right up ladies and gents, step right up!

Ah Fung: (In Cantonese.) How do you plan to get away with that?

Rebecca: NEXT! WHO'S NEXT?

Fanny: (In Cantonese.) Missus had a breakdown...

Rebecca: Ah Fung!

Ah Fung: Yes Missus Loo-zee?

Rebecca: Call me Rebecca

Ah Fung: Yes

Rebecca: Becca

Ah Fung: Yes

Rebecca: *Rebecca*

Ah Fung: Yes

Rebecca: Ah Fung, I want us to be honest. We've known each other a long time

Ah Fung: Long time Missus Loo-zee

Rebecca: You never liked him

Ah Fung: Who Missus Loo-zee?

Rebecca: Joe! You never liked him, you *don't* like Joe, you *hate* him, you *fucking* hate him!

Ah Fung: (In Cantonese.) Strong words...

Rebecca: No, I hate him too! Joe was attractive *sure* in the beginning. Idealistic kid from the middle of fucking England with the hipster beard, pristine Mick Jagger impersonation and the big dreams. I'm going to be a writer Rebecca! I'm going to see the world live like fucking Orwell in fucking down and out Hong Kong! Took me in with them. Took us

88

all in with them, Elaine, Ricky, we all thought *he*'s making his life happen. But he's a liar. He's a liar in a second-hand, second-class suit. Sleeping around. Snorting dope. Sad sad sad and we haven't had sex in, he stopped, he's stuck, fallen off the ladder. I'm ascending, ascension to higher planes, higher being, making shitloads of money. Did I mention I make shitloads of money? Yeah. SHITLOADS. And, and I'm happy. REALLY FUCKING HAPPY!

Ah Fung: (In Cantonese.) You deserve better than Joseph Losey.

Rebecca: My mouth is dry, very dry. Could you, can you get me some water please?

Ah Fung: (In Cantonese.) Get her some water.

Fanny goes to the kitchen, fills a glass, hands it to Hitler.

Fanny: (In Cantonese.) Be useful. Take this over to the boss. Go on.

Hitler hands the glass to Rebecca. She takes a sip.

Fanny stuffs her mouth with a slice of pizza.

Fanny: (In Cantonese.) I *will* be getting paid in cash right?

Ah Fung: (In Cantonese.) I wish I could record every word that comes out of your mouth Fanny.

Ah Fung takes out his cigarettes, pauses, looks at Rebecca.

Rebecca: Go right ahead Ah Fung.

Ah Fung: Thank you Missus Loo-zee.

Fanny: (In Cantonese.) Smoking's bad for you.

Rebecca: Smoking'll kill you.

Ah Fung: (Laughs.) I try to stop once. I fail!

Rebecca: Becomes a habit.

Ah Fung: Mm. Helps me think.

He lights up.

*On one side of the room Hitler begins rooting through the cardboard box marked "**ROB HUNTER: EDITOR**".*

Rebecca: What's he got over there?

Ah Fung: Wai, Hitler!

Hitler ignores him, finds the BB gun, pockets it quickly as Ah Fung walks over to him.

Ah Fung: Ah! Mista Hunter's old things.

Rebecca: Bring it here Ah Fung?

Ah Fung brings the box over to Rebecca. Hitler runs to the door - opens it - it's Ricky.

Ricky: Hiya Hitler.

Fanny: (Mouthful.) Hallo hallo!

Ricky gives a short nod, walks in. Meanwhile Rebecca continues to pull out a few news clippings, photos...

Rebecca: Crap...crap...crap.

Ah Fung: Good evening Mista Ricky. You are early.

Ricky: Ah Fung. Don't tell me she didn't give you the day off? Thou doth protest not enough.

Ah Fung: Missus Loo-zee is very tired. Come back later.

Ah Fung tries to block Ricky's path to the living room. They do a little dance, back and forth, side-to-side.

Ricky: (Exasperated.) Bloody hell!

Ricky passes him - finally.

Ricky: (Laughs.) Forget none of you can walk in a bloody straight line!

Ah Fung: Sorry-ah.

Ricky: Rebecca, are you...?

She takes out a framed photo, pauses -

Rebecca: "Happy families"!

She throws it onto the floor, continues to rifle through the box, pulls out a document. After a moment she begins laughing hysterically.

Ah Fung: Laughing is good for you, for heart!

Rebecca: Can you believe *him* of *all* people forgot to make a will! I had this brill idea of scattering his ashes over the South China Sea, should've seen the lawyer's face (beat.) I never once questioned or complained about his lack of affection, overbearing expectations, affair after affair behind my mother's back but he always held this resentment for me being here. Hypocrite. I remember his stories, stories of growing up with nothing, stories of escape from home. We had a laugh. And he did try, he did try very hard to accept me marrying Joe, "the university drop out with the dodgy accent". How did he...? By moulding him. Not as far as making him into a version of himself. Worse. He *bought* him. Only thing that was mine, ours...this flat. Look at it Ah Fung, in its irreversible state of disrepair!

Ah Fung: I drive Mista Hunter many years and always, he *always* say he angry with himself that he never remember to say how hard you work. He was proud of you.

Rebecca: He said that? Robert Hunter said that, with no bitter sense of irony?

Ah Fung: What is "irony"?

Rebecca: My entire life story!

Ah Fung: Right before, he say vewy odd thing to me. He say "Hong Kong all dressed up with nowhere to go."

Fanny: (In Cantonese.) I don't geddit.

Ah Fung: (In Cantonese.) You wouldn't.

Rebecca: I've figured it out Ah Fung.

Rebecca's mobile. [hidden beneath debris on the coffee table] goes off.

Fanny: (In Cantonese.) Not mine.

Rebecca: I married my father!

Ricky: You gonna get that?

Rebecca shakes her head.

Ricky: What's the matter Becs?

Rebecca: Head'll be fine once I've taken a moment

Ricky: To?

Rebecca: Think. Be. Shower. Douse myself in Chanel No. 5. Never look half-decent till I've got my armour on.

Ricky: You always look beautiful, with or without.

Rebecca: So much to do! This place, positively uninhabitable. Unvarnished floors, unpainted walls, nails poking out from every crevice, god when will it end? Those limited edition bar stools atrocious I know, I should really take those back but since we will only be able to afford "IKEA" now! Caterer not here? Better call Ah Fung!

Ah Fung: I am right here Missus.

Rebecca: Right. Yes of course you are. You drove me home.

Ricky: Where were you?

Rebecca: Around

Ah Fung: Missus Loo-zee's club call me

Ricky: What can I do?

Rebecca: Leave me alone

Ah Fung: You betta go Mista Ricky

Ricky: No mate you better

Ah Fung: You cannot say when or where I go. Missus Loo-zee my employer.

Ricky: Becca? Becca, please tell Ah Fung to mind his own business.

Rebecca: Hell hath no limits, where hell will ever be...no that's not it.

Ricky: Lets get you up and -

Rebecca: Lets *not* Ricky. I'm tired, so tired.

Ah Fung: You see Mista Ricky?

Ricky: Yeah I see, see you taking *advantage*

Ah Fung: You will be late!

Ricky: Late for what?

Ah Fung: March for freedom. March for vote.

Ricky: Rebecca needs me

Ah Fung: Missus Loo-zee will be fine. I take care. You go!

Ricky: Not gonna leave her here mate!

Ah Fung: You peepoll. Chi seen! You think she future of Hong Kong?

Ricky: This isn't your problem Ah Fung.

Ah Fung: She all mix up!

Rebecca: Hong Kong needs a hero. Why are you here Ricky?

Ricky: What are you gonna do about Joe?

Suddenly Hitler and Fanny begin fighting - he runs into the bedroom, Fanny runs after him.

Rebecca: In my mind London buries, consumes. Was that the only solution? He wanted to -

Ricky: To escape the bubble

Rebecca: "See the world"? Fact: he failed. Fact: he blames me.

Ricky: He's stopped blaming you

Rebecca: Joe reached out to *you*? That's funny. That's very very funny.

Ricky: Time to bury the hatchet Rebecca. No mans an island. You can start over.

Rebecca: shakes her head, tearful. She holds onto him. He pats her gently.

Ringing continues.

Rebecca: Fuck (beat.) Off.

Ringing continues.

Ricky: You can start over.

Ringing...

Rebecca: Fuck (beat.) off.

Ring ring...

Rebecca: Bugger off!

Knock on the door.

Fanny: (In Cantonese.) Oh my god! Who is that? Is that the police?

Knock knock knock.

Ah Fung: (In Cantonese.) Did you call the police?

Fanny: (In Cantonese.) No, but...

Fanny opens the door. Joe and Elaine enter.

Ah Fung: Mr. Loo-zee! I never get you call. I would have pick you up.

Joe: I went native Ah Fung

Fanny: Native? Wah, "natave"?

Joe: (To Fanny.) Hello again "Amah."

Fanny: Hallo hallo!

Aside:

Fanny: (In Cantonese.) Hate to say I'm enjoying this but I am.

Ah Fung: (In Cantonese.) *Shut up* Fanny!

Ricky: Mate.

Joe: Shouldn't *you* be "pounding the streets"?

Ricky: Yeah

Joe: "Giving a shit"?

Ricky: Yeah Joe I was *about* to -

Rebecca: What brings you two back to Chez Tai Ping Shaan sans Shaan?

Rebecca attempts to stand...fails.

Rebecca: Here for one last "hurrah"?

Joe: No need, want, sense of triumph. No win or lose.

95

Rebecca: Then?

Joe: One last

Rebecca: Don't bother!

Elaine: We were worried

Rebecca: Poor you

Elaine: Rebecca

Rebecca: *Elaine*

Elaine: Rebecca

Rebecca: *Elaine*

Elaine: Rebecca have you eaten? How about a nice cup of tea?

Rebecca: Always with the tea and sympathy! I'm sick of it. I'd rather a, a shot of I don't know. I just don't know. I want to get up. I want to -

Ricky: Give me your hand.

Ricky puts out a hand to her. She doesn't take it.

Rebecca: You're fired.

Ricky: Right

Rebecca: Sorry

Ricky: OK

Rebecca: That it?

Ricky: Pretty much

Joe: Look, d'you mind giving me and my wife a bit of privacy?

Rebecca: I totally *totally* get it now.

Joe: Glad you "geddit" now?

Rebecca: *You're* the reason I'm going to have to leave! Can't stick around this "jukejoint" anymore. Lost face, lost...you've put into motion my demise, was it difficult to bear? This heavy burden, scraping, fighting tooth and nail down to the beds, rubbed raw to ruin my reputation? *How* tedious, standing, waiting in the wings for the opportune moment. She's vulnerable, why not fill her up to the brim some more?

Elaine: She's drunk

Rebecca: Sobering up now thanks to you. I for one, would like to know what she thinks about all this.

Rebecca stands, points to Fanny.

Fanny: Wah?

Rebecca: (To Fanny.) What do you think about all this?

Fanny: I no understand!

Rebecca: Was it as good for you as it was for me?

Elaine: Stop harassing the girl! She doesn't *anything*

Rebecca: Oh I think she does. YOU KNOW EXACTLY WHAT'S BEEN GOING ON HERE DON'T YOU?

Fanny: (Frightened.) I, I no understand!

She backs Fanny into a corner.

Rebecca: You will serve as the unprejudiced "local local" opinion here. Help me make my mind up (slowly.) Do you understand?

Elaine: Sounds like your mind's already made up

Rebecca: Forgive forget move on move out, away from you, from here, from this hole I've buried myself in. How could I ever think I'd be the one? The one to hoist

97

the flag, the freedom flag. Hong Kong will one day be free, I'd be free! Silly silly me.

Joe: Are you saying

Rebecca: Yes

Joe: Rebecca!

Joe goes to embrace her, she moves away.

Rebecca: There's something else. Something I can't quite put my finger on.

Joe: What is it?

Rebecca: I don't know. Yet.

Joe: Well

Rebecca: Not going back to London

Joe: You've made that very clear

Rebecca: Wanted to be clear this time

Joe: I want you

Rebecca: Unconditionally?

Joe: I love you!

Rebecca: What's wrong with me?

Joe: There's nothing

Rebecca: Not enough

She begins unbuttoning her blouse.

Joe: What're you doing?

She takes off her shoes.

Rebecca: This. Do you like this?

She begins performing a mock-striptease.

Joe: Stop it.

She continues, laughs. Joe, exasperated-

Joe: Stop it.

She ignores him.

Joe: You always have to have an audience Rebecca! Our whole marriage -

Rebecca: Isn't that you like Joe? Spotlight on.

Joe: Fine. You want a confession? Fine. I confess, I'm the dick who cheated on you with -

Elaine: Joe *don't.*

Ricky: Christ.

Pause. Rebecca roughly kisses Joe, pulls away.

Rebecca: You were lonely, you did a stupid thing, you were remarkably drunk, spur of the moment, in a drunken stupor. You had a few, more than a few but it won't happen again, it will *never* happen again.

Elaine: Joe and I will *never* happen again.

Rebecca: Did you scrub him off you every night before bed? Did you scrub your skin, hands, neck, shoulders, parts of you he touched until it bled? How long?

Ricky: Rebecca this isn't like you to -

Rebecca: Oh go find a bong to smoke. How long?

Elaine: I'm ashamed of what I've done

Rebecca: You haven't done a thing love, don't worry about it! You weren't the first you know. you were convenient. Yes. Convenient fuck for him - convenient friend for me.

Elaine: You've always run away from the present, lived in the past.

Rebecca: Was it out of a misplaced yearning for the "other", the "different"? That's often the rationale in these cases, my father for instance, par excellence of familial fuckups, his mistress had the balls to text my mother on all the sordid details but you two have been friends for god knows fucking ages so...so *poignant*, "good for the soul". That's what you always say isn't it? Simultaneously spouting half-rhymes to half-people in half-rooms. Hey, we've finally met halfway Elaine!

Ricky: That's unkind

Joe: She was kind to me. She was home when I didn't have one.

Elaine: He left to end it

Rebecca: No. He ran!

Elaine: If you knew

Rebecca: We see love quite differently don't we?

Elaine: We do

Rebecca: We never had anything in common did we?

Elaine: Not really

Rebecca: Not until Joe

Elaine: He's come back to you hasn't he?

Rebecca: (To Joe.) Do you love her?

Suddenly - Fireworks explode in the distance.

Rebecca: Do you?

Fanny: (In Cantonese.) What the hell was that?

Fireworks continue...

Fanny and Hitler reenter from the bedroom. They run to the balcony.

Rebecca: Scratch the surface, what will you find?

Fanny: (In Cantonese.) Oh my god! The fireworks are way better from up here!

Rebecca: Drum roll please!

Fanny: Ooooooooooooowaaaahhhhhhhhhh!

Rebecca: That's it, that's the spark.

Ricky: Meaning?

Rebecca: I've lost.

Elaine: You haven't lost anything

Rebecca: If that's what you think "Gwei-Pour".

Elaine: You're not tied to any one thing, one place, one colony, one country. I think, no I *believe* you've got the best of both worlds and you have an opportunity now to -

Rebecca: Next you'll be telling me that you're proud of your title, of the *filth* you roll around in!

Fanny: (In Cantonese.) Not again!

Near the balcony - a scuffle ensues between Fanny and Hitler. She is attempting to take the BB gun back away from him.

Fanny: (In Cantonese.) Give that back to me you little shit!

She chases him around the living room.

Rebecca: Why isn't anyone here yet anyway? Ah Fung, what's the time?

Ah Fung: (In Cantonese.) Stop acting like a fucking idiot Fanny!

Rebecca: Ah Fung?

Fanny: (In Cantonese.) Who, me?

Ah Fung: Yes missus?

Rebecca: Doesn't he have a home to go to? Unlike the rest of us. Kitty! Winnie! Whatever your name is. Take him home, take him would you? Take him away.

Ah Fung: Nobody home. Nobody care.

Rebecca: Everything's as *usual* then. Everything, everyone in this god damn city is as usual. We'll go back, as if nothing's happened

Hitler runs behind Ricky.

Ricky: I'll take the little tyke home

She walks over to the stereo, turns it full blast - begins dancing.

Rebecca: You have bloody hands, wash them!

We hear the sounds from the Prologue simultaneously with the firework display.

She stops dancing right in front of Joe, reaches into his trouser pocket, pulls out the pill bottle.

She offers a few to Joe - he shakes his head. She washes down a few pills with the booze.

Rebecca: (Sing-song.) Send her victorious, Happy and glorious, Long to reign over us, God...god...god...save...save the...queen.

Fanny: (In Cantonese.) Mental. Bloody mental. Like they'd really leave behind this penthouse flat with the million dollar view and the live-in maid.

Ah Fung: (In Cantonese.) You're too young to understand. Live a little then come back to me.

Fanny: (In Cantonese.) They're a bunch of freeloading expats! Think they're so lucky to get that coveted luxury free pass to the "orient", ticket into the most respectable "members only" clubs Hong Kong has to offer but after a while, after say, a year they won't be able to think about anything else (beat.) And who wouldn't? Being able to afford what most of us can't even imagine, impromptu trips to their own private island, golf on the fake astro turf imported from three different continents, countless parties hosted by the elite laid out on a silver platter, but they pay the price I mean, they're limited by, confined to the streets of Soho, Lan Kwai Fong, Lyndhurst Terrace (their stomping grounds) they avoid Wanchai like the plague because its branded (apparently) the lower class kind of place where only Australian losers like him hang out. They never venture out to eat locally and their food is imported from Finland!

Ricky: Denmark actually.

Fanny: (Surprised.) Yes! Heh...

Rebecca picks up the pill bottle, begins playing with it.

Joe: You don't have to, to prove anything to me.

Rebecca: But I want to, I wanna be "part of the club" and if that's the way it has to be. Welcome home darling!

Rebecca swallows a few more pills. Sounds from the Prologue [in reverse] grow even louder alongside the sound of the fireworks and the classic tune "Highland Cathedral."

[Prince Charles]: "This marks a moment of change and continuity in Hong Kong's history..."

[Thatcher]: "Naturally..."

[Ricky] "Fuck if I know whether its better or worse since 1997."

Ricky: You're not making any bloody sense. None of you are making any sense!

Elaine: I need a drink.

Rebecca: In control, out of control.

[Prince Charles] "We shall not forget you..."

[Soldiers] "FORWARD MARCH!"

Rebecca: Can be anyone you like. Escape who you are.

Hitler runs over to Rebecca.

Fancy: (In Cantonese.) Oy! Get back here!

Joe: My home, my roots, they're just stories inside my own head. They manifest themselves in the way I see them. Do I "love" love? Is holding onto the memory of home, loving this feigned image of a loving hearth, of a place where you come from like a, a sort of perversion? Then I guess I'm pretty fucking perverted then but don't let that put you off too much, I'm hopeful too. "To go home is to go back to where you came from". To root yourself somewhere, or that root you severed...you can, you will reconnect with again. I'm rootless too Rebecca. Does that mean I'm damaged? In case you hadn't noticed there's a huge tattoo on my forehead, it reads "already-damaged". No seriously. I can't stop myself from saying to you what I am, I can't help myself. But I know you feel that way too. I know it. Don't you, don't sometimes feel that way?

Rebecca: As if love, as if home has damaged you for good?

Joe: Yes, yes exactly.

Rebecca: Someone said the way we love, the way we express is fragmented so when we say we love someone what we really mean is we love them now but that could change at any time, at any second. Truth. Bottom line. You don't know what it is you're looking for.

Joe: So help me Rebecca

Rebecca: Like a child

Joe: Help me to be a better man.

Rebecca: What is "home" anyway? Don't they say "home is where the heart is"? That's what they say isn't it? Fuck homes. Fuck hearts. Going home for some people, cathartic, explosive, like really good sex or that song you can't get out of your head but for me, it's nothing. Nothing.

[Chris Patten] "Unshakeable destiny..."

[Thatcher] "Again and again and again"

Rebecca: Born again.

[Prince Charles] "Her majesty the Queen...good wishes...staunch... special friends...

[Margaret Thatcher] "Its almost a miracle..."

Joe: Rebecca...

[Ricky] "Ten years on...the rebirth...what a load of shite..."

[Thatcher] "We negotiated...we hope it will be upheld...again... again... again and again..."

Joe: Please.

Rebecca: Long to reign over us!

Joe: I *need* you.

[Chris Patten] "This is a cause for celebration...not sorrow..."

Joe: Can you hear me? I said I *need* you.

Rebecca: Guests should be arriving soon...

[Ricky] "You're listening to the Enquirer news radio service with me Ricky Forrester..."

Rebecca: Was that the door? Is someone at the door?

Ricky: I think we're alone

Elaine: All alone

Joe: Not alone.

Elaine takes a swig.

Elaine: Isn't that what being human is all about? Being alone?

Rebecca rises.

Rebecca: I'm going...

Joe: Going?

Rebecca moves to the door - opens it.

Rebecca: But the place I'm going. Not a place, more...a new way of seeing.

Hitler appears, aims the gun at her.

Rebecca puts up her hands in surrender.

The stage is flooded with red light.

Hitler pulls the trigger - CLICK.

The End

HONG KONG ARTS FESTIVAL (HKAF)

香港藝術節於 1973 年正式揭幕，是國際藝壇中重要的文化盛事，於每年 2、3 月期間呈獻約 150 場演出及約 250 項「加料」和教育節目，致力豐富香港的文化生活。

香港藝術節是一所**非牟利機構**，約三成經費來自香港特區政府的撥款，約四成來自票房收入，而餘下約三成則有賴各大企業、熱心人士及慈善基金會的贊助和捐款。

香港藝術節每年呈獻眾多**國際演藝名家**的演出，例如：芭托莉、卡里拉斯、馬友友、格拉斯、馬素爾、沙爾、巴里殊尼哥夫、紀蓮、史柏西、皇家阿姆斯特丹音樂廳樂團、聖彼得堡馬林斯基劇院基洛夫樂團及合唱團、巴伐利亞國立歌劇院、紐約市芭蕾舞團、巴黎歌劇院芭蕾舞團、翩娜·包殊烏珀塔爾舞蹈劇場、雲門舞集、星躍馬術奇藝坊、皇家莎士比亞劇團、莫斯科藝術劇院及北京人民藝術劇院等。

香港藝術節積極推介**本地演藝人才和新晉藝術家**，並**委約及製作**多套全新戲劇、室內歌劇和當代舞蹈作品，甚或出版新作劇本，不少作品已在香港及海外多度重演。

香港藝術節大力投資下一代的藝術教育。「**青少年之友**」外展計劃成立 23 年來，已為約 700,000 位本地中學生及大專生提供藝術體驗活動。藝術節每年亦通過「**學生票捐助計劃**」提供近 9,000 張半價學生票。

香港藝術節每年主辦逾百項深入社區的「**加料節目**」，例如示範講座、大師班、工作坊、座談會、後台參觀、展覽、藝人談、導賞團等，鼓勵觀眾與藝術家互動接觸。

HKAF, launched in 1973, is a major international arts festival committed to enriching the life of the city by presenting about 150 performances and 250 PLUS and educational events in February and March every year.

HKAF is a **non-profit organisation**, with about 30% of annual revenue from government funding, around 40% from the box office, and the remaining 30% from sponsorships and donations from corporations, individuals, and charitable foundations.

HKAF presents **top international artists and ensembles**, such as Bartoli, Carreras, Yo-Yo Ma, Glass, Masur, Chailly, Baryshnikov, Guillem, Spacey, the Royal Concertgebouw Orchestra, the Mariinsky Theatre and Valery Gergiev, Bavarian State Opera, New York City Ballet, Paris Opera Ballet, Tanztheater Wuppertal Pina Bausch, Cloud Gate Dance Theatre, Zingaro, Royal Shakespeare Company, Moscow Art Theatre, and the People's Art Theatre of Beijing.

HKAF actively promotes **Hong Kong's own creative talents and emerging artists**, and **commissions, produces and publishes new works** in theatre, chamber opera and contemporary dance, many with successful subsequent runs in Hong Kong and overseas.

HKAF invests in **arts education** for young people. In the past 23 years, our **Young Friends** has reached about 700,000 secondary and tertiary school students in Hong Kong. Donations to the **Student Ticket Scheme** make available close to 9,000 half-price student tickets each year.

HKAF organises over 100 **Festival PLUS** activities in community locations each year to enhance the engagement between artists and audiences. These include lecture demonstrations, masterclasses, workshops, symposia, backstage visits, exhibitions, meet-the-artist sessions, and guided tours.

如欲**贊助或捐助**香港藝術節，請與藝術節發展部聯絡。
Please contact the HKAF Development Dept for sponsorship opportunities and donation details.

電郵 Email dev@hkaf.org	直綫 Direct Lines (852) 2828 4910/11/12	網頁 Website www.hk.artsfestival.org/en/partner

香港藝術節
Hong Kong Arts Festival

地址 Address:	香港灣仔港灣道2號12樓1205室 Room 1205, 12th Floor, 2 Harbour Road, Wanchai, Hong Kong	出版：香港藝術節協會有限公司 承印：香港嘉昱有限公司 本刊內容，未經許可，不得轉載。
電話 Tel: 2824 3555	傳真 Fax: 2824 3798, 2824 3722	電子郵箱 Email: afgen@hkaf.org
節目查詢熱線 Programme Enquiry Hotline: 2824 2430		Published by: Hong Kong Arts Festival Society Limited Printed by Cheer Shine Enterprise Co., Ltd Reproduction in whole or in part without written permission is strictly prohibited.

職員 Staff

行政總監 Executive Director
何嘉坤 Tisa Ho

節目 Programme

節目總監 Programme Director
梁掌瑋 Grace Lang

副節目總監 Associate Programme Director
蘇國雲 So Kwok-wan

節目經理 Programme Managers
葉健鈴 Linda Yip
梁頌怡 Kitty Leung

助理節目經理 Assistant Programme Manager
余瑞婷 Susanna Yu*

助理監製 Assistant Producer
李宛虹 Lei Yuen-hung*

節目統籌 Programme Coordinator
林淦鈞 Lam Kam-kwan*

節目主任 Programme Officers
李家穎 Becky Lee
林晨 Mimi Lam*

物流及接待經理 Logistics Manager
金學忠 Elvis King*

藝術家統籌經理 Head Artist Coordinator
陳韻妍 Vanessa Chan*

外展 Outreach

外展經理 Outreach Manager
李冠輝 Kenneth Lee

外展統籌 Outreach Coordinator
李詠芝 Jacqueline Li*

外展主任 Outreach Officers
陳慧晶 Ainslee Chan*
黃傲軒 Joseph Wong*

特別項目統籌 Special Project Coordinators
巫敏星 Maria Mo*
馬彥珩 Peggy Ma*

特別項目助理 Special Project Assistant
林己由 Kayol Lam*

技術 Technical

技術經理 Technical Manager
溫大為 David Wan*

助理製作經理 Assistant Production Manager
蘇雪凌 Shirley So

技術統籌 Technical Coordinators
陳寶愉 Bobo Chan*
陳詠杰 Chan Wing-kit*
陳佩儀 Claudia Chan*
關玉英 Dennes Kwan*
蕭健邦 Leo Siu*
歐慧瑜 Rachel Au*
梁雅芝 Shirley Leung*
張鎮添 Timmy Cheung*

技術主任 Technical Officer
梁倬榮 Martin Leung*

出版 Publication

中文編輯 Chinese Editor
康迪 Kang Di*

英文編輯 English Editor
黃進之 Nicolette Wong*

助理編輯 Assistant Editor
王翠屏 Joyce Wong*

市場推廣 Marketing

市場總監 Marketing Director
鄭尚榮 Katy Cheng

市場經理 Marketing Managers
周怡 Alexia Chow
鍾穎茵 Wendy Chung
陳剛濤 Nick Chan

助理市場經理（票務）
Assistant Marketing Manager (Ticketing)
梁彩雲 Eppie Leung

助理市場經理 Assistant Marketing Manager
梁愷樺 Anthea Leung*

市場主任 Marketing Officer
張凱璇 Carla Cheung*

票務主任 Ticketing Officer
葉晉菁 Jan Ip*

客戶服務主任 Customer Service Officers
吳靄儀 Crystal Ng*
唐力延 Lilian Tong*
謝家航 Alex Hsieh*
張蕙莉 Ridley Cheung*

發展 Development

發展總監 Development Director
余潔儀 Flora Yu

發展經理 Development Manager
蘇啟泰 Alex So

助理發展經理 Assistant Development Managers
陳艷馨 Eunice Chan
陳韻婷 Alyson Chan*

發展主任 Development Officer
黃苃姍 Iris Wong*

藝術行政見習員 Arts Administrator Trainees
譚樂瑤 Lorna Tam*
梁斯沅 Miri Leung*

會計 Accounts

會計經理 Accounting Manager
陳綺敏 Katharine Chan

會計主任 Accounting Officer
張清婷 Crystal Cheung*

會計文員 Accounts Clerk
黃國愛 Bonia Wong

行政 Administration

行政秘書 Executive Secretary
陳詠詩 Heidi Chan

接待員／初級秘書
Receptionist / Junior Secretary
李美娟 Virginia Li

*合約職員 Contract Staff

督印人 Publisher	何嘉坤 Tisa Ho
主編 Editor	蘇國雲 So Kwok-wan
執行編輯 Executive Editor	余瑞婷 Susanna Yu
助理編輯 Assistant Editor	王翠屏、李宛虹 Joyce Wong, Lei Yuen-hung
平面設計 排版 Designer	羅美儀 Paula Law
攝影 Photographer	Calvin Sit
出版 Published by	香港藝術節協會有限公司 Hong Kong Arts Festival Society Limited
印刷 Printer	嘉昱有限公司 Cheer Shine Enterprise Co. Ltd.
版次 Edition	2014 年 2 月初版 1st edition, February 2014
書號 / ISBN	978-988-16056-7-2
定價 / Price	港幣 HK$120
版權垂詢 Copyright Enquiry	香港藝術節協會有限公司 Hong Kong Arts Festival Society Limited

香港灣仔港灣道二號 12 字樓
12/F, 2 Harbour Road, Wan Chai, Hong Kong
電話 Tel : 2824 3555
傳真 Fax : 2824 3798, 2824 3722
網頁 Website : www.hk.artsfestival.org
電郵 Email : afgen@hkaf.org

FILTH © 2014